JUST ONE *Spark*

Author of the Kiss Me Crazy Series

JAMI ROGERS

For Alyssa, Christian, Megan, and Trisha,
I hope all women have friends as beautiful inside and out as
the four of you.

Just One Spark

Copyright © 2017 by Jami Rogers

All rights reserved.

This is a work of fiction. Names, characters, businesses, places, events and incidents are either the products of the author's imagination or used in a fictitious manner. Any resemblance to actual persons, living or dead, or actual events is purely coincidental.

Editor: Julie Sturgeon, CEOEditor, ceoeditor.com

Copyediting/Proofreading: Casey Dawes, Concierge Self-Publishing, www.ConciergeSelfPublishing.com

Visit my website: www.authorjamirogers.com

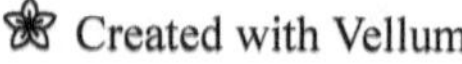 Created with Vellum

JUST ONE *Spark*

JAMI ROGERS

JUST ONE SPARK

THE BLACK ALCOVE SERIES BOOK 5

ROGERS JAMI

CHAPTER ONE

Beth

I haven't had sex in more than a year. Tonight, I have every intention of changing that. All the late nights of studying, constant emails with professors over assignments or potential careers, and leaving work or barbeques with friends early to make sure I'm getting everything with school finished have finally paid off. I've landed my dream job and it's time to celebrate—but more importantly, relax. And what better way than with some good old-fashioned one-night stand sex?

That should be easy to do, too, since I'm in Rockland, Colorado, visiting my good friend Liam—who, thankfully, is the only person here who knows me—and not back home in Wind Valley, Wyoming. Although, I'll be headed back tomorrow to prep for my first day as a working woman. It's a long stretch to get an assistant to the marketing director position straight out of college, but I'll be damned if I'm going to let all that hard work go to waste.

I scan the inside of the bar, searching for the perfect fling material. I come up short of prospects, taking in the fact it's only six in the evening and there aren't very many people here. There's a group of women in the corner near the bathroom hallway, wearing pastel pink, blue, and green dresses that just scream spring. Only two of the four pool tables lined against the back wall are being used, and there's a couple sitting at one of the round tables in the middle of the open room. Not a lot of choices for me at the moment.

"All I'm saying is that it's a risky move," Liam says. He's the manager, working behind the bar tonight at the Silver Tap. It's the sister bar to the one where I work in Wind Valley — now only weekends—The Black Alcove. That means free drinks for me. This is perfect, because as much as I am mentally shouting, "Yay, one-night stand," I'm also mentally shouting, "Don't do it. STD." Vodka and the splash of cranberry in front of me is definitely going to make one of those thoughts disappear. I mean, it's not like I'm going to go find the grimiest guy in the bar. I have standards, even if I say shit, fuck, and speak my mind way more than a person should. I don't really have a filter, but that has nothing to do with how I pick my men.

"I want to get laid, Liam. Since you and I have no attraction whatsoever, a stranger is going to have to do," I tell him. But I also prefer it this way. I want sex, not a relationship. Easy as that.

Liam squeezes his eyes closed and turns away from me. Probably thinking of how he attempted a night of lust but I just couldn't do it. Yeah, he's just under six feet, all muscle, and dark hair, dark eyes, but I don't know ... maybe it's because I was friends with him first. That and my refusal to commit to a man—even when we go months without keeping in touch—could cost us our friendship. Anyway, every now and then, by the way he brushes an arm against me or voices his concerns about me always being alone or how I should see someone about my hesitation to jump into an actual relationship, I still think he has a thing for me. A small thing—I hope.

He releases a long sigh as he busies himself making drinks from the tickets he just tore off the printer. "At least pick the guy here, all right? Then I can see his face and maybe card him for his drink to memorize his address or something before you leave with a complete stranger who could murder you in the back of his car."

"First of all, I still have those handcuffs you gave me at Christmas." I pause, letting him laugh it off. It was a gag Christmas gift. Well, so he thinks. I really do plan to use them one day. "And second of all, you're being dramatic. That's not going to happen."

"You don't know that." He isn't laughing anymore.

"Considering I am planning on using the bathroom here or my room at your place, since that is where I'm staying, I do know."

"The bathroom, Beth, really?" he asks.

"At least you'll know where I am." I grin at him. I'm trying to help the guy release some of his discomfort with my evening plans. His lack of a smile says I'm not doing a good job.

A customer walks up a few stools down and Liam excuses himself to take care of the bald-headed man.

My phone lights up, as if my mother knows I have a free moment and was going to use it for something illicit. I let it ring.

It's not that I don't want to talk to her, but I don't exactly have the patience for it right now. If she wants to talk about something other than my dad, sure, I'd love to chat. But ever since my dad started dating someone new, she's been extra needy. Not to mention her drinking has increased. Right now, I want to tell her to suck it the fuck up. *You've been divorced for ten years. He's allowed to date again and so are you.* But of course, I'd never say any of that. My parents are the perfect example of why commitment is bullshit.

"So, tell me again how this new job works. They don't just hire you?" Liam asks once his customer has left.

"Yes, I'll going into the office every day and earn a paycheck, but I'm on a ninety-day trial. So yeah, if I don't earn the position, they let me go."

I really hope they don't.

"Do a lot of places do that?" he asks.

"I think it's more popular with bigger companies."

"What are you going to do if you don't make it?" he asks.

I sit up with my arms crossed in front of me. "What do you mean *if*, Liam? They'll keep me."

"But what if they don't?" he prompts.

"I need a new subject," I blurt out. "You're depressing me with your lack of excitement and clear confidence in me." Instead of the small sips I've been taking, I start to gulp down the remainder of my drink. It would be fantastic if this liquor would work faster.

"Hey, I'm thrilled you got this marketing job. I know you've been working hard for it and I'm sure you'll keep it, but sex with a guy you don't know seems like a pretty manly way of celebrating."

"Whoa, sexist. What are you trying to say?" I unintentionally slam my glass against the counter.

He releases another sigh as the entrance door opens, streaming in the last little bit of daylight over his face as the sun is beginning to go down.

"Nothing. I take that back. It's just an odd way to handle victory is all," he says.

Victory.

I let the word settle in as a group of rowdy men step inside the bar. They're all donning suits and ties. But they look young. Possibly somewhere around my own age of twenty-five. Thirty, max. One man stands out in the crowd, not only because he's the only one to wander to the music box, but because he is the only one who has well-groomed scruff that covers his face. It's shaved so perfectly that his jawline is more pronounced than normal. I've never been a fan of facial hair, but tonight, I think I could be.

He taps away at the screen, searching for what I hope is a song I'll enjoy. After all, he did just cut off the playlist I lined up on the damn thing. Took me over an hour, too.

Bands. Every bar should stick to live bands.

He shifts from his right foot to his left, sliding every finger but his thumb into his right pocket. His left thumb of his other hand rests against his lips as he pauses. I like those lips. They aren't too plump and they aren't so thin that I'll feel like I'm kissing his chin more so than his mouth. They look like nice kissing lips. His tongue glides over them, leaving a glistening coat. Yes, those are positively kissable lips. I'm still staring when he turns. He must have sensed he was being watched because a pair of bold, golden brown eyes settle right on me. He smiles and then winks. I twist back around to face Liam.

"Looks like you found your guy," he says, full on rolling his eyes at me like a girl.

"No, I'll keep looking," I say.

"Why? He is clearly into you?"

"Yeah, he also caught me looking at him, which means he thinks I'm into him, which also makes him think I'll be easy."

"But you're specifically searching for a man to have sex with. What am I missing here?" Liam asks.

"Yeah, well I still want the guy to work for it. I mean this" —I point to my face and my body—"is not just something you get. You have to earn it." I'm not conceited, but I know every woman, beautiful or flawed, deserves to be wooed properly. No matter the circumstance. And tonight, even though I'm not going to focus on any part of my life but sex, I still want to feel wanted by whoever I choose. The trick now is finding the right guy and turning tonight into one of the best nights of my life.

Maverick

"You slept with our client's wife."

My father, who doubles as my boss, paces behind his desk. He's not asking a question. He already knows the answer. It's more like he's waiting for me to confirm the accusation. Which I will, because it's true. I just hate that I've disappointed him. Again. It's like senior year when I told him I wanted to follow in his footsteps in the family marketing business instead of taking the college football scholarship in Tennessee. Most fathers would have been thrilled. Not mine.

He had to have known I would make that choice. He interned me with the company every summer since eighth grade, and some nights after school, we'd sit and spitball ideas back and forth for hours. I never did it as an excuse to spend time with him after mom died in my junior year of high school; I did it because he loved it, and because he loved it, so did I. So now I'm here, eight years later, working with him and struggling to accept that what I did shouts how much I haven't grown up.

"I didn't know she was his wife. Most wives attend the meetings instead of waiting in reception," I say.

His stride stops and he turns to face me, leaning forward, palms flat against his desk. "You cost the company a seven-figure deal, Maverick."

He had to remind me. I've beaten myself up more than anyone over this since six days ago when this same mentioned woman came into our office, bringing her husband to meet me so he'd know she wasn't lying. I'd say they had some problems going on at home and I was her ticket out. But no matter their issues, I'm the one who made the mistake.

"Had I known who she was, it wouldn't have happened." I lean back in my seat, cross one ankle over the opposite knee, and loosen the collar of my shirt. "You know I would never intentionally cost us a contract."

Closing a seven-figure deal will always get my blood pumping. No matter how many times I've watched the owner of a company sign his name after I've pitched him the most brilliant marketing proposal he'll ever hear, it never gets old. I'm not a cocky jackass like most people think; I'm just good at my job. Extremely good. Others—coworkers, friends, people I meet in passing—choose to call me a jerk rather than admit they wish they could do their job the way I do. I have a

95 percent success rate. Who doesn't want to say that about themselves?

Most people think I'm in this position because my own father is the president of this company, Mitchell Marketing. The degrees hanging on the wall behind my desk in my office say otherwise.

"No, no I don't know that. Not with these juvenile actions," he says.

His hard stare matches my own.

"Dad, I've closed more contracts than almost everyone here combined. Not including you, of course."

Great, now I'm mixing a little bit of whining with bragging. This is not my style.

"Sealing the deal doesn't mean anything if you don't have respect for our company. This business wasn't created for our kids to come in here and tarnish the hardworking and loyal reputation we've built."

"That's all Austin's doing," I say. My cousin is a spoiled idiot who blows through my uncle's money doing everything he can to avoid growing up.

"After this stunt, I'm not so sure he's alone."

"Dad—"

"Maverick, I've always known you love marketing. I knew you'd be great at making the pitch to our clients and that you'd be the best man to replace me as president when I retire, which is why I hired you as soon as you had your degree. But now, I'm not so sure I made the right choice."

"Whoa, Dad, I messed up. I know I did, but you don't need to fire me." I sit up, resting my arms on my thighs. "I'll find a way to make back the number we lost. You can trust me."

A sly smile crosses my father's lips, the same one he used to display after my games in high school when he'd hear people talking about what a great arm I had. He's always loved knowing something other people didn't.

"I know I can, and that is exactly why first thing Monday morning, you will start new hire recruitment for the assistant to marketing director position in Wind Valley under your uncle's guidance."

I sleep with a client's wife and instead of punishing me, he sends me to Wyoming to choose who the next person we hire is?

"Uncle Bart wants me there?" I ask. I haven't seen the man since my graduation. Talked to him on the phone and emailed him through the company for business, yes, but on a personal level, no. And not once in any of our work conversations did he show any type of acceptance of me. Mostly because I was able to skip the recruitment phase myself. I got lucky. Although, I have no doubt I would have come out as the best recruit for whatever job they were hiring for at the time.

"Of course he does. In fact, he was the one who mentioned the idea to me," Dad answers.

"Wow, I don't know what to say. I'm honored you have that much faith in me. I won't let you down. I'll pick the best candidate." I stand, straighten my tie, and turn for the door.

"Maverick."

"Yeah?" I twist back around.

"You're not going to be selecting a recruit."

"I'm not?"

"No, you are one of the recruits."

I blank on any response.

"Prove to me and this company in the next ninety days that you want to be here and I'll bring you back to Colorado. You can resume your current position as VP project director, and we can discuss the idea of my retirement in the next couple of years. If you don't succeed in earning your place back, then you no longer have a job here."

"I made one mistake; it's not going to happen again," I repeat myself.

"Then you should have no problem proving that to everyone else in the company who will one day, hopefully, look up to you as an employer." He nods, once, his clear tell sign that this discussion is over. I return his nod and again head for the door.

"One last thing," his voice stops me. "You've got to start placing the needs of the company before your own in certain areas. Your love life and career need to be fully separate. Mixing the two is the perfect recipe for disaster."

"Yes, sir," I say with no hesitation and finally leave his office.

Don't worry, Dad. If mixing sex and business together is going to set me back every time, I can guarantee it will not happen again.

I follow a group of men inside the bar. The men, like me, are all sporting suits. I've heard that downtown Rockland includes more office buildings in a five-block radius than most other cities in the northeastern part of the state. The Silver Tap, the bar I'm walking into right now, is conveniently in the middle of those five blocks. Whoever opened this business right here knew the opportunities a placement like this would provide them. The average working human enjoys a drink after work. This location is a brilliant move if you ask me, considering I fall into average right now.

The crowd that enters in front of me veers to the left, claiming the table nearest the door. I take a quick scan of the room. I'm meeting my sister, Tiffany, for drinks, possibly two. She wants to talk about what happened. Not as head of human resources but as my sister.

I spot a jukebox out of the corner of my eye and head that direction. I press a few buttons and ponder my choices of music: country, rock, rap, and more. It's a basic selection. I settle on some oldies. A rack of pool balls breaking rattles behind me. A round sounds like a great distraction, considering my sister is going to jump right into the discussion of what she thinks I should do when I get to the office on Monday.

I look over my shoulder to see if there is an empty pool table, but I don't get a chance to find a free table before a solemn woman with fiery red hair who's seated at the bar grabs my attention. She's staring right at me and doesn't even flinch once I send her a wink and grin. All things considered, finding a random hookup isn't the best choice to make right now, but hell, I may as well go all out tonight if I'm going to be all business for the rest of the summer.

Red's expression doesn't change before she twists back around. The bartender braces his arms against the bar top before saying something to her.

She flips her hair over her shoulder where it ends gracefully at the middle of her lower back. She wearing black shoes that could easily be mistaken for socks. Her dark blue jeans are ripped at the knees and her black t-shirt barely meets the waistband of her pants. She looks over her shoulder once more and I barely catch the spark of emerald in her eyes before she reverts her gaze forward again.

My type has always been suits and success, but something about this woman won't let me pull my eyes away.

"Can I get you something?" a blond waitress in a navy mini skirt asks.

"No, I'm all right. Thanks. I'm just going to have a seat at the bar," I answer. She nods and passes me on her way to her next table.

There are about ten empty barstools at the bar, but I head straight for the one beside Red.

The bartender shifts away from her to greet me. "What can I get ya?" he asks.

"I'll take a Coors Original, please," I say and steal a glance at the woman next to me.

She makes a gagging gesture with her finger before she turns to me. "Of all the beers you could pick, you pick the most repulsive one available."

I chuckle. "And what would you have recommended?" The bartender hands me my beer and I take a swig, waiting for Red's answer.

"Maybe a Sam Adams or something else not so boring."

"Boring," I repeat. "I've actually never been told that my taste of any kind is … boring."

Her lips twitch right before she licks them and narrows her eyes at me. I hadn't been expecting her to be so quickly responsive to my comment.

"I take it we've moved past talking about beer," she says.

"Well, did you want to continue small talk or get right to point of why I sat next to you?"

Her gaze flashes between me and the bartender, who is now at the other end of the bar and not paying attention to us.

"I'm going to step outside for some air. Would you like to join me?" she asks, spinning on her chair and standing.

I chug the remainder of my beer and rise. "I'd love to."

Ninety-five percent perfect success rate.

I follow behind her, catching the moment she glances back to the bartender, again. I do the same and am struck by his posture—arms folded across his chest and a glare. Perhaps I should be worried that I'm about to steal another man's woman for a bit, but if they were actually together, he would have been over the bar top by now with his fist in my face. I mean, if I had a girl who looked like the one with the swaying hips in front of me, I'd work overtime to make sure men knew she was mine.

We step outside and Red heads straight for the side of the building. The second I turn the corner she pushes me up against the faded red brick. I expect her to dive right into kissing me, but she doesn't. The way her sultry eyes roam over my body makes the decision of what to do next for me.

My lips capture hers and my tongue invades her mouth before she can protest. Bracing my hands on her hips, I spin us around. I lift her and she wraps her legs around me before it's her turn to be pressed against the wall.

Her hands rest on my face as she kisses me harder. Her fingers curl in my hair, and the way the tips massage my scalp each time her tongue collides with mine sends a newfound sense of desire from my head all the way to my toes. The evidence of how much I'm enjoying this presses against her stomach, only fueling her kisses. We're basically rubbing against each other where anyone can see us. A pinch of jealousy that someone could see her like this when it should be meant only for me runs through my body. No woman has ever given me a single thought even close to that one, and I pull away.

Warm eyes gaze up at me. I lean down to kiss her once more and then release her legs till her feet are planted back on the ground.

Red bites her bottom lip and the action makes me dip to take over for her. I could kiss her all day long.

"Your place or mine?" she says before I get the chance.

A woman who knows what she wants. Man, this one just keeps getting sexier and sexier.

"If we exchange names, that might—"

"Make things complicated," she finishes for me. "Look, if you don't want to do this, I don't care."

"No, I do," I say a bit too eagerly. I take her hand and start to lace our fingers so I can lead her back to my place—probably the worst idea I've ever had—a couple blocks away when she jerks her hand away from my touch.

"Sex. Just sex. No hand holding or anything else."

"It was an innocent move," I say, holding back a laugh.

Instead of taking off for my place, I press my body into her, my legs parting hers as I lean forward, kissing just under her ear.

"I don't want commitment. If you're looking for one night with a guy who will treat you right and put all your needs before his, I'm your man. I've never been arrested and I have a clean bill of health. I'm twenty-six and my name is—"

"Stop." She holds up a hand and smiles. "The less we know about each other, the better."

A smile tugs at my lips. "Really, no names?"

"No names," she repeats.

She full out wants to have a complete one-night stand. I'm not sure whether I should be appalled or impressed.

A growl comes from deep in my throat as my lips devour hers again. Her head falls back the best it can as I kiss down her neck to her chest. I lift one leg to my side, allowing myself to grind into her, a preview for later.

Later must not be something she wants, because her hands glide under my jacket and before I know it, she has unlatched my belt and pulled down my zipper.

"You can't be serious!" Both Red's body and my own freeze at the high-pitched shrill behind us. "I'm ten minutes late and you've already moved on to new plans for the night."

I immediately twist my body to shield Red and the display of my very pronounced erection.

"What are you doing? Oh, my god!" My sister yells one more time as she observes me and Red with a furious gaze.

"Tiff, stop yelling" is how I start but am immediately cut off from saying any more.

"You have a girlfriend!" Red scolds and shoves me back.

"What?" I ask and jerk my pants back into place. "No ... I—"

"You're a pig," Red snaps, yanking her shirt back down.

"Wait," I call out just as she is almost around the corner. "I don't have a girlfriend. That wasn't—"

"Yeah, clearly you don't now that she caught you."

"No, I mean, can we just try this again?"

My sister lets out a huff as she crosses her arms, glaring at

Red while she watches our interaction. That certainly doesn't help.

"You're kidding, right? One-night stands are supposed to be easy. This was a train wreck, and thank fucking god I never have to see you or your girlfriend again. All girls deserve more than what your sleezeball ass has to offer."

With that, she marches back inside the bar.

I slouch back against the wall. Well, that was a disaster, but I can't say it was the first time that's ever happened to me. It is, however, the first time I want to tell my sister to fuck off.

"Mav, you can't be distracting yourself with a woman right now. Might I remind you that's how you got yourself into this mess?"

I press the heel of my palm into my eyes. "It was just sex, Tiff."

"I'm sure it was," she says, placing her hands on her hips as she glares at me. "You want the president spot, you need to be focused."

"If I want sex in my life, Tiff, no one is going to tell me I can't." I push off the wall and look down the street. I'll need another bar if I want some drinks.

"Mav," she says, her tone laced and ready for an argument.

"Tiff." There isn't anything she can say about this entire situation at work that I haven't already told myself.

We have one of our typical brother sister stare downs that usually end with her winning. Not this time.

"Fine," she snaps. "You're right."

"I know I'm right," I say. She shoves me as we walk away from The Silver Tap.

"You might be a little right, too," I say. "I've let Dad down enough this last week. I don't plan on doing it again."

"Ever the family man, that guy," she replies. "He just wants what's best for you, Mav."

It's true, Dad is all about running a successful business, but he's even more about having a family. He wants it for both of his kids, but neither of us have made that commitment yet. And I sure as shit haven't been going about it the right way.

I take a look over my shoulder as we make our way down the street. I could go back, explain Tiff is my sister, and probably get back to where I left off with Red, but that's a lot of work for one night of sex. And besides, I need to focus on developing an approach to the next three months. I'm not letting this job slip out of my hands. That's what I should be worrying about, not thinking about how the most gorgeous woman I've ever met now thinks I'm the world's largest scumbag. I should probably just pretend this evening never happened and feel lucky that the chances of ever seeing her again are slim to none.

CHAPTER TWO

Maverick

Day one is off to a complete shit start.

I step off the elevator onto the third floor where the firm is located and everyone who is within sight is gaping at me. A few are looks of pity, a few look irritated, and only one looks happy. Ann, the company's receptionist who used to work out of the Colorado office, has a bright smile on her face as she greets me. She also dated my father for a year or so. When they broke up she transferred here. Their situation is a good example of why my father is against a relationship that involves anything to do with the workplace.

"Maverick, how are you this morning?" she asks, her tone laced with a hint of curiosity. I glance around at the cubicles and offices in the quiet room. Almost everyone has resumed their focus on something other than me.

"I've been better, and yourself?"

"I'm well, thank you. I'll be honest; it's really nice to see you, but I wish it were under better circumstances," she says.

I give her my best smile and nod. I couldn't agree more. Starting over is not what I had planned for the next three months. "So, where am I going first today?" I ask. I don't want anyone to think I'm going to take to the easy way out. There isn't one, even if I were searching for it.

"Your uncle asked me to show you to the office you'll be using while you're here. He's in meetings all morning and won't be able to visit with you until this afternoon." She adjusts her skirt as she rounds the side of her desk.

"At least I still have an office," I say, a lame attempt at a joke that only gains me a look of sympathy from Ann instead of the laughter I was aiming for.

"It's a joint office," she says, keeping her focus in front of us. "You'll be sharing with one of the other temp hires."

It doesn't surprise me that my uncle Bart would put me in a joint office. But with only one of the two of my new coworkers is odd.

"Why not both?" I ask.

She pauses in front of a door and waves me in. The gray walls are cold and empty aside from a couple pieces of art, the desk, and the three chairs around it. The blinds aren't open, so I move to change that. A little sun through the windows will help.

"Your cousin, Austin, is the third new hire," she says.

I spin around from adjusting the blinds. She can't be serious. Austin has been riding his trust fund for years. He's never had any intention of working in the family business. Like my uncle, it may have been a few years since I've actually spoken with him directly, but I can't imagine much has changed.

My face must say enough of what I'm thinking because she adds, "Your uncle says it's because he's ready to straighten up. But between you and me, I am certain Bart didn't give him much of a choice."

"And if he doesn't?" I ask.

She shrugs. "I have no idea."

"Well, this summer should be interesting," I say.

"Oh, I have no doubt about that, Maverick. The young woman who is also working with the two of you was the top of her class. She came with very high recommendations. We are all very eager to see what she can bring to the table."

"I, too, was at the top of my class," I say with a smirk. Anyone who loves what they're learning and what they want to do can make it to the top of their class.

"I know you were." She laughs. "How could I forget the excitement in your father's face the day he watched you graduate from CU?"

She squeezes my arms as she heads out of my office. "Don't get into too much trouble before the meeting. I'm rooting for you, you know."

I take my seat behind the desk. The black leather chair is chilly under my suit. I open a few drawers; there isn't even a pen included. From the sound of it, I'll have enough time to head down to the supply room and get everything I need. I glance at the adjoining door to the next office. Working with someone who sounds like she wants this job as much as I do will either make it easier to get through the next ninety days or harder. Either way, between her and my cousin, it's safe to assume she might be my only competition.

"Knock, knock," my cousin, Austin, says as he does exactly that against my door. "You're getting rusty on showing up early in the morning, cousin," he says.

"It's not even eight yet," I say, already frustrated just by his presence. "I'd say I'm fine." His overly highlighted blond hair appears as if it's glowing from the light through my shades.

Working with my cousin should be great, but it's not. I went to college and graduated with a degree in marketing. My cousin … well, I'm not sure what he did in college. He was only there because my uncle made him go by telling him he would revoke his trust if he didn't. I have landed more deals than everyone at the company except my father and my uncle in just the two years I've been here. I'm made for this job and have no idea why my cousin would be interested in a career after all the years he's spent without one.

"Dad and I were here before everyone. You know that's what it takes to make it as boss here, Mav. If you're not going to fill the part, I think it's time you let your father and mine know you can't handle it."

He may be family, but fuck if he isn't the most conniving little shit I've ever met. Chances are, he was here early only because my uncle has threatened something he wants once again. Bribery is the easiest way to get Austin to do anything.

"Is there something I can help you with?" I ask.

"I'm serious. You're not doing anyone any favors by sticking around when you don't want to be here," he says.

"Are we talking about me or you?" I ask. Without me here, he'd actually have a chance. With me in the running, it's going to prove how wrong he is for this business.

His eyes match my own glare as he flips his jacket back on one side and sits on the edge of my desk. "Should we talk about this girl who is starting today? I mean, can you even handle her being in the office next you?"

"Austin," I warn him.

"Hey." He stands with his hands up. "I didn't force you to get involved with the last one who landed you here. So don't get an attitude with me."

"I'm not going to discuss this with you." It's not up for argument. I won't let the same mistake as last time happen. My eyes flash to the door with a small tick of my head, hinting it's time for him to leave.

Austin's departure is like watching a kid leave the room after his parent just confiscated his toy.

"Just don't screw it up again. Our fathers' company can't afford for you to make us look like fools the way you did.. My grandfather didn't build this place just for you to show the world you can't work side by side with a woman."

Our grandfather, I want to correct him, but I don't. He doesn't even know what he's talking about.

My chair bounces off the wall behind me as I stand with a rush. He thinks he's doing right by this company, but he's not. He's wasting our time and money by being here.

I don't have time to deal with Austin and the drama he has decided to bring to work.

I'm going to get my job back and never let my dad down again. That's the goal, and I won't let anything get in the way of making my career the one I deserve it to be.

Beth

The scent of evergreen wafts in front of me as I wait behind Ann's, the receptionist's, desk. A man in a suit has his back to me, but if I didn't know any better, I'd say he is my "attempted" one-night stand. *Wow.* Now I'm imagining him. This is not a good sign. It's not even nine a.m. yet.

"Mr. Mitchell asked that I give you a tour and show you where your office will be. It's nothing grand, but it's where we put all our new employees. Once you hit the ninety-day mark, we'll move you to a room with a view." Ann beams at me and I reciprocate. She did say once I hit the mark, so I think it's safe to say she believes I've got this.

"Follow me." She waves her hand as she takes off down a long hallway. Offices on the left have windows and on the right there are cubicles. *Please, don't give me a cubicle.*

I move to follow her when a deep-throated chuckle halts me. Is that …? Noooo. I look behind me, but the guy still has his back turned. *Shit.* That sleezeball must have done a number on me if I think I can hear him now, too.

"So this will be yours." *It's on the left.* I pinch my lips together to hide my smile. I have an office, with a small window no less. This makes it like super official. *Look at Beth everyone, all grown up.* Will I get a nameplate and my own phone? And yes, I hope I get business cards.

I step inside, not caring even the slightest that this space is about one-fourth the size of all the other offices. A metal desk sits in the middle, meaning my back will face the window. The walls are white, and only one has anything on it. It's a framed picture with two giant M letters diagonal from each other. The words Mitchell Marketing is printed in small letters at the bottom.

The company's logo.

"What's with the extra door?" I ask. It reminds me of conjoining rooms in a hotel.

"You'll be working directly with Mr. Mitchell's nephew, Maverick." She clears her throat and pinches her lips together. I almost want to laugh at her failure to hide her smile. "The adjoining offices make work easier. You'll see," she says with a wink.

"Is he a coach of some kind?" Why would I be paired with him?

"No, he's also under a ninety-day trial."

I'm working against family?

Fuck.

"When will I get to meet him?" I need to see what I'm up against as soon as possible.

"This afternoon, at the meeting where you and the others will be introduced to everyone."

"Others?" I'm trying my best not to show my clear concern. I'm also struggling not to let the word *fuck* slip every time she reveals something that's beginning to make my nerves shoot out the window.

"You, Maverick, and Mr. Mitchell's son, Austin," she says, and I don't miss the sad smile she fails to hide.

Double shit. There is no way I'm going to make the cut. I can't compete with family. It's like I'm being set up for failure.

"That sounds … wonderful," I say and when Ann laughs and pats my shoulder, heading for the door. At least one person will understand my sarcasm.

"Anything I need to do before then or anything I need to know?" I ask.

"Oh yes." She thumps her forehead with her palm. "Sam from HR will meet you within the hour to go over new hire paperwork. I'd try to complete it all before the meeting; the Mitchells will more than likely want to jump right into work on the new client you three are to represent today."

"I can't wait," I say, and this time, there is no sarcasm. I really am looking forward to working here. I just have to show them I am the best and everything will be fine.

"One thing you should know about Maverick." She hesitates in the doorway. "He takes his work extremely seriously." Her voice is soft and kind, almost like a mother asking for you to be patient with her child.

"Well, then, we will get along great," I tell her.

"I sure hope so," she says with a tight-lipped, forced smile. "Enjoy your morning and welcome to the company."

I watch as she leaves before exploring my work space. I slip off my jacket and look behind the door. No hook, but shit yeah, a mirror.

I look smart.

I twist to the left. *Looks good.* I twist to the right. *Looks good, too.* My heather-gray pencil skirt and cream sleeveless frilly blouse give the illusion that I have more sexy curves than I ever thought I would have in my life, and my boring black heels enhance the good all that running at the gym has done for me.

My hair is curled down to the middle of my back—I haven't done anything other than straighten it in years. My makeup is the best I've ever seen, and I honest to god don't even look like me. Jeans, t-shit, and Converse. That's me. This, the woman looking back at me, is Beth 2.0.

I take my seat behind my desk and take a deep breath. I have ninety days to show these people that I am the right woman for this position.

First rule and probably the most important: do not say *shit*, *fuck*, or any other of my favorite foul words. I no longer work full-time in a bar setting, and I pray for all those who are willing to help me control my swearing habit.

Second, smile. It's not that I lack the ability to form this feature on my face, but really, I should do this more. Third, always remember my please and thank yous—this one will probably be the easiest for me. My parents—as messed up as they can be—raised me with manners. Fourth, make friends but don't seem so outgoing that people think I'm here more to socialize than I am to work. I need my coworkers to enjoy being around me. If they like me, perhaps they'll keep me.

This is just like the first day of school. Except this time around, I'm willingly putting myself in a "you don't know anyone, but you're going to be great" situation.

I press my lips together to hide my smile and pull my phone from my purse. I don't care how unprofessional this is, but I have to send my girlfriends, Sara, Kelsey, and Sky, a picture of my office. Better send one to Abby, too. Then I'll start the paperwork that will lead to the best career ever. I'm going to succeed. I just know it.

CHAPTER THREE

Beth

My chair and computer are angled perfectly to my door. Anytime someone walks in, I don't have to twist, scoot, or lean in any way to see them. I just have to look up. And that's exactly what I've been doing every single time a person walks by my door. Not a one stops in, but the movement keeps drawing my gaze, and it's driving me insane.

I'm not waiting for anyone to greet me. I'm not expecting anyone to come in here and want my opinion right away. However, it would be nice, considering Ann and Sam from HR are the only people I have met so far. I know she said I wouldn't meet the guys I'm working with—or against depending on how you look at it until this afternoon's meeting, which is … I click the side of my phone till it lights up with the time—exactly five minutes from now. Aside from the part where I have to be introduced to everyone, I'm eager to be assigned my first project. I've done nothing this morning but fill out the typical new hire paperwork. Harassment rules, insurance information, retirement plans, dress work standards. This is definitely the least fun/cool part of the job.

"Hey, Beth, do you want to walk to the meeting together?" Ann asks, poking into my office, leaving only her head and left shoulder visible.

"Yes," I answer and stand, straightening my skirt and blouse. I grab the notepad she gave me earlier and a pen.

Both Sara and Kelsey are going to go out of their minds with excitement over my new job. We're all living the lives we talked about as little girls, Sara owning her father's bar and turning it into a small chain across Wyoming and Colorado, Kelsey writing her heart out as a bestselling author of supernatural romance, and now me, the marketing girl.

I can't tell you exactly how I fell in love with marketing, but it had something to do with the fact I watched TV more for the commercials than the actual shows. Skip-It commercials hooked me—kids laughing and skipping one leg at a time, the ball at the end lit up in bright colors. I begged my parents to get me one every night when that commercial came on. Just that thirty-second clip excited me. Eventually, I got a Skip-It for Christmas and I loved it, but then the next cool toy came on television and I was sold. Both on the toy and on what I wanted to do when I grew up. Showcasing something so that every time its name is even mentioned, you smile and think, "Yup, I need to have that." I want to give that to people.

The conference room is at the end of the hallway. It's in a large room on the corner of the floor, leaving two walls filled with floor-to-ceiling with windows. The view over the town is incredible. Even though the building is on the outskirts of the eastside of Wind Valley, away from where I live and the bar, I can still see the trees that make up the park in the center of town. Wyoming is such an eye-catching bright and green place. I can't ever imagine living in a big city and not having access to this type of beauty every day when I walk out my front door.

A long table filled with chatting employees sits in the middle of the room. The plush large chairs surrounding it, at a glance, look as though they could seat about thirty people. I follow Ann down the side near the window, nodding and smiling at those already seated as we pass. The door clicks closed loudly just as I take my seat.

"I apologize for my tardiness," the man says. I glance up to the clock. He's right on time. I know right away this is Bart Mitchell. His short trimmed white hair and mustache match his online photo perfectly. Right down to the scar above his left eyebrow. Unfortunately, I didn't get to interview with him because his schedule was too busy around that time. He can't be much under six feet tall. His suit is a bit snug on his large frame, but something about the way he holds his shoulders back as he scans the group in front of him brings my focus to his eyes. The way they narrow hints that he's waiting for everyone's full attention.

"Although we are waiting on a couple more, let's get started," he says.

Everybody adjusts in their seats to face the table, pens in hand, ready to take notes. I do exactly as they do.

"First, let's start by welcoming Beth Moyer to the group. She's just finished her master's in marketing, and today she has begun her trial period with Mitchell Marketing along with Maverick and Austin, whom everyone already knows. Beth, would you come up here?" He holds out his hand, even though I'm obviously too far to grab it. I stand, unsure of why

I have to get up. I'm clearly the only new person here. But I do it anyway, with a smile. *So far, so good.*

I hold that smile as I walk back down the row of people. My lips are almost shaking with how hard I'm trying to hold the smile. Then the door opens and everyone looks away from me. I follow their gazes to welcome the distraction.

Everything happens in slow motion. My smile falters then my step does, but I'm still walking. My eyes are wide, and my heart is beating at a lightning pace. I can't peel my eyes off the door.

Fuck.

There, standing in front of me with the biggest grin I have ever seen on a man, is my "almost" one-night stand. I can see his smile and I can see him waving; it's when his lips start moving that I blink.

"My apologies for being tardy," he says, directing his attention to Mr. Mitchell.

Holy shit. What is he doing here? I was in Colorado, not here last weekend.

"I'm glad you could join us, Maverick," Mr. Mitchell greets him. "There is a seat in the back next to Miss Moyer here. I'm just doing a quick introduction before we begin."

This is Maverick, the one I share an office with? They have got to be fucking kidding me.

Maverick brushes past me, never taking his eyes off mine. He even turns to walk backward as he makes his way to his seat, and dammit, I'm twisted around now, watching over my shoulder.

Shit.

I am so totally and completely screwed.

"Miss Moyer." Mr. Mitchell's booming voice is finally

able to pull me out of the daze I've fallen in. "Why don't you tell us a little bit about yourself?"

I look out at the pairs of eyes now focused on me. My eyes dart immediately to one set and I have to force myself to look away before I can speak.

"My name is Beth Moyer," I begin, and cringe when my eyes find his again. "I moved to Wyoming at a young age." Maverick leans back in his chair, resting one ankle over the other knee as he watches me. The smug smirk on his face ignites something inside me. Just because I tried to sleep with him doesn't mean I have to get all tongue tied over it. I am here for my job and nothing else. Five minutes of distraction is all he gets. From this moment on, he gets nothing from me.

"I graduated from the University of Wyoming Online with my master's in marketing. I have an intense drive for success, and I believe that all ideas can be made into something that can make history. I have confidence in Mitchell Marketing to encourage me to make those ideas happen for not only myself but those around me. Failure isn't an option for me, and I enjoy helping others whenever I can, so please, know my door is open to anyone for any reason." I nod, dismissing myself back to my seat before I'm asked to say more.

Luckily, Mr. Mitchell doesn't comment on my self-introduction. Instead he thanks me and goes straight into business. It's the best meeting ever, minus the part where Maverick and I spend most of the hour stealing glances. He with amusement and me with frustration.

Finding a one-night stand was officially the worst idea I've ever had, and my morning pep talks are about to have a whole new meaning.

.   .   .

Maverick

I'm a confident man. I do the research, I put in the time, and I make sure my facts are on point. Yet the biggest challenge I think I'll ever face at this company is sitting right next to me. As if thinking about her nonstop for the last three days wasn't bad enough. I was thankful to get here this morning for a distraction, ready to regain my focus where it needs to be, but now she's here. She's a coworker who will work directly with me. In the office right next to mine. I've thought about women before, but never has one captured my attention the way Beth has. There is a chance that this offer to redeem myself just got a little harder.

I'm not some sap who believes in fate, but fuck if her showing up today doesn't make me start. Maybe my mom had been on to something with her "meant to be" crap. The only downfall now is that we work together. I clearly know better than anyone else how dating a coworker or someone closely related to the business can set you back. And if I don't choose my actions wisely, Beth could be the biggest setback of all.

Fuck.

When the meeting is dismissed, my uncle asks me to stay behind to have a word. I want to tell him that I've heard it all already and that I don't have time to be reminded of my mistakes once again, but my father wouldn't like that. As much as I don't want to admit it, if my father believes working under my uncle is the right move, so do I.

When Jeremy, the last employee to leave the conference room, is out of the door, my uncle turns to me. He flicks back the sides of his jacket, placing his hands on his hips as he pins me with a hard stare. His nostrils flair just barely and a wrinkle forms between his eyes.

"Do not mess this up."

He's referring to a whole lot more than just work with those five words.

"I won't."

"Maverick, I mean it. I want to help your father out, but you have to be willing to do the same."

"I am. It's going to be fine." My attempt to reassure him does nothing.

"You're going to be sharing an office space with Ms. Moyer. Is that going to be a problem?" he asks.

"No," I answer quickly and confidently. The way he and my cousin talk to me, you'd think I'd slept with the whole goddamn company.

"She could have picked a job anywhere, but she chose here. Don't give her the impression that she made the wrong choice."

I hold back the groan struggling to break free. Being reminded of this one situation is getting old. I'd tell him that, too, but as my superior, that move wouldn't end well for me and it sure wouldn't show my father I'm taking responsibility for what I did.

"Whatever happened between the two of you when you walked into this room needs to end here, too," he says.

"Whoa, she hasn't even been here five minutes."

"I don't care. I've seen that look only once before. I better not see it again."

"What look? When?" I ask, confused and not exactly sure we're on the same page at the moment.

His brow rises and his head tilts right as he hits me with a stern look.

"You can trust me," I say, my voice strong as I return the

gaze. "My goal is to move myself and the company forward, not back, sir."

Neither of us moves as we face each other. This happens a lot with my dad, too. Only then, it's the worst seconds of my life while my father tries to decide whether or not he believes me.

"I'll meet you all in Beth's office in ten minutes to go over a few things. The rest of what I'd like you to complete in the next few months will come in an email by the end of the day." He nods, looking past me. I turn to see Austin with a satisfied grin. It's like working with a teenager who just wants to stand around and cause drama.

Against my better judgment, I head straight for my office. I close the door behind me and then proceed to open the one that leads to Beth's. Her hair falls over her shoulder when she quickly looks up. She's writing something at her desk. I'm curious as to what it is since we haven't started on anything yet.

I reach her door and close it, too. I twist to face her and find her making her way around her desk. Her hands fidget with her skirt. She's smoothing it out, but all I see is the curve of her ass better than before. I'm a little taken back at how quickly she is walking toward me, a determination in her eye that only confirms that what I feel toward her is matched all the way.

I reach to stop her so I can tell her that what happened over the weekend can never be mentioned or reenacted—I think she is planning that right now—because my job depends on it, but she dodges my touch, moving for her door instead. She opens it, wedges the stopper into place, and then glares at me before returning to her seat.

"Don't ever come into my office and close my door without my permission."

I may have misread her actions just now. By a lot.

"We need to discuss business," I say and begin to remove the doorstop. She jumps from her seat.

"We can do that with the door open."

"Okay, we also need to discuss a few other things," I say. Her flustered tone makes me want to laugh. Which kind of makes me a dick. Or, really, I'm sure it does since I shouldn't find her frustration attractive.

"We have nothing to discuss." She practically kicks the rubber wedge under the door. "And please, leave my door open."

"All right, the door stays open." I can't help but smile.

It can't be a good trait to know that just being near her, even though she clearly wishes I weren't here, which, ironically, is what I should want, puts me in one of the cheeriest moods I've ever had.

I take a seat across from where she sits behind the desk. Of course, she hasn't looked up. It's a clear sign she wants me to go, but let's face it, that isn't going to happen anytime soon. We were just given the TACM 110.4 Music to the Max radio station account. Spending time together, a lot of time, is a given at this point.

Since she isn't looking at me, I take this moment to observe her. I can't decide who is sexier: the laid-back, torn jeans, and t-shirt Beth with perfectly messy hair and an attitude that lets a man know he's in for a tough time, or sleek, dressed up Beth with heels and shiny, straight hair who now full of determination. I find both very intriguing and attractive. But we're strictly work buddies. It's my only option.

"I'm glad to see you here," I say. "I …"

"I don't think your girlfriend would like you making that comment," she cuts me off, still not looking up.

"That wasn't my girlfriend. It was my sister. I don't have a girlfriend," I say, grinning as I wait for her response.

She continues to focus on her desk, but I see the way she bites her bottom lip.

"I suppose …"

"Of course you're already in here," Austin says, strutting into Beth's office, narrowing his eyes at me and taking the seat next to mine. "I'm Austin." His attention is already on Beth. "The boss's son," he adds like it should explain everything about him. He doesn't even offer to shake her hand.

"A pleasure," she responds, leaning back in her seat. Her gaze flickers between Austin and myself. I'm smiling because this is a good sign that her spitfire attitude isn't just for me. Working with her might be more fun than I expect.

"Perfect, you're all early," Bart says, closing the door behind him. Beth and I both straighten in our seats while Austin continues to look bored.

"As you know, you are going to be working with TACM on their new marketing plan," he repeats. "This is going to be more than a six-figure contract if you can finalize the deal. I'll be observing the three of you closely." He pauses, something catching his eye. Austin is sitting next to me, drawing on his notepad. I'm surprised he even brought one. "I'll be watching your ability to work quickly and efficiently. The way you represent the company. How you work together in a team environment as well as individuals," Bart says, clearing his throat. Austin looks up. "That means *all* of you. Teamwork is supported greatly here, so I'd suggest working as a team for the pitch. However, if you decide to divide the project, you can decide responsibilities among yourselves."

Beth is scribbling quickly on her notepad.

"Unfortunately, we can only keep one of you at the end of the trial period. I wish you all the best of luck. Your first piece of the project should be in your inbox as we speak. Enjoy the rest of your day," he says and leaves.

Beth speaks up first. "I think we should give the teamwork thing a try."

"I agree," I say.

"I'll probably be better off without the two of you" is Austin's reply.

"I understand, but perhaps we should give the first task a try as a whole, and if you feel it doesn't work for you, then we can split it," Beth suggests.

"Whatever. I'll be in my office—let me know what you want to do first," Austin says before leaving.

"I sense working with him is going to be a blast," she says, and I chuckle.

"You have no idea. I'll go read over the email and message you my ideas."

"Great."

I head for the adjoining door, pausing to look over my shoulder.

She stares right back at me. She doesn't say anything and neither do I.

The word *interesting* just took a whole new meaning at work.

CHAPTER FOUR

Beth

Maybe marketing isn't the job for me after all. I jam the gearshift into park and head inside my apartment. I mean, if it were the job for me, wouldn't I have had the most memorable first day ever?

Technically I did, just not in the way I wanted.

When I walk through the door I'm greeted with silence, and inside I'm screaming *thank god*. Just a few minutes of alone time, sitting on the couch with my eyes closed, is exactly what I need right now.

My roommate, Abby, is always open to sharing her opinions whether you ask for them or not. And nine out of ten times, they are the worst or most stupid thing I've ever heard. She wasn't my first choice to move in with me, but alas, I needed the rent money and I was tired of losing roommates I actually liked, so I chose her. That's not to say I don't like Abby, but the girl has definitely got a screw loose. Or ten. Or all of them. I have commitment issues, and Abby *is* the commitment issue.

Right now, though, I really need some time to hear myself think because, let's face it, I'm not quitting. I want this job and, aside from working with Maverick, I think I'm going to really enjoy my time there. The problem is, how do I do it without wanting to throat punch him for how ashamed he made me feel that night or without trying to throw myself at him again? Somehow, behind all my annoyance, I still find him devastatingly gorgeous. Three different sex scene scenarios crossed my mind while he was in my office this afternoon. The one with him pressing my front against the wall while his body and hands explore mine from the back popped up when he marched over and closed my door without saying a word. Had I not opened it, I couldn't promise I'd have held myself back from making one of those scenarios come true.

My cell rings and I eye the name that appears on the scene. Mom again. I silence the call. I have way too much going on to deal with her.

I let out a long and very dramatic sigh. What is going on with me? I don't fantasize about men like this. It's like my mind is screaming, "Be a lady!" while the rest of my body is screaming, "Take his clothes off!"

Shit, each time he spoke with that deep, throaty voice of his, all I heard was a voice that was up to no good and could force me to make bad choices. A voice that, had he commanded, would have made me do anything he wanted.

I am so totally screwed. Not just over him but the whole situation. I can't compete against the boss's nephew and the son. There is no way the company will pick me over either of them.

"Hellllloooo," Abby singsongs as she walks through the door. Poking her head around the wall between the kitchen and the living room, she smiles. "Tell me all about your day."

I groan, loudly.

"That bad, huh?" she asks.

"It was worse than bad."

Her brow raises and she leans against the wall with her arms crossed.

"There is this guy I'm working with who is a fucking scumbag and I have to work directly with him," I tell her. "It's going to be a long three months."

"Geez, that's twice in one week I've heard you complain about a guy. By your tone, I can't decide which one you dislike more, the scumbag from work or the sleezeball from the weekend."

She looks at me, her head tilting as she taps her foot.

"If you must know, the man is one and the same."

"What? I thought your days of one-night stands were over," she says.

I knew I shouldn't have said anything to her. It was a weak moment, but she wouldn't leave me alone until I filled her in on my weekend.

"It was an attempted one-night stand," I correct her, "and even if I had gone through with it, doing it again with him would be a horrific idea."

"Why not? I do it all the time," she says, and I honestly think she's expecting a real answer. "And now he's like, always accessible when you need to get some."

Abby is the most promiscuous girl I've ever met, and she

couldn't care less what people think of her. Well, I think she cares more than she lets on, but that's another story. I may be blunt, but I care. Some days I wish I didn't, because it would be easier and take away some stress. Not that I have much to begin with, but landing this job would be a lot less stressful if I didn't give a damn.

"My way is the fun way," she adds.

"Your way is the trouble way," I say.

"And what about this guy is trouble?" she asks.

Nothing can really be defined as trouble to Abby. I know this because I used to think the most heartless people on earth were the cheaters. My dad did a fine job of teaching me that. He also, by lying to my mother and leading her on for a few years, taught me to develop a no nonsense approach to life. Abby though, Abby keeps reminding me that the second most heartless person is the one who helps someone cheat. If you can fall that far more than once in your life, you clearly don't care about trouble. I'm blunt because I hate bullshit and too much bullshit leads to trouble, among other things—like believing something that isn't real.

"Fuck. All right, where to start? Hmm, he's the boss's nephew," I tell her.

"Eh, it could be worse." She shrugs.

"My office has a fucking adjoining door with his because I work directly with him."

"I still don't see the problem, but yes, yikes. See, I told you it could be worse." She pushes off the wall, talking as she heads for her room. "As you can gather, I don't have much advice for you other than just have sex with him and get it over with. You'll be less tense about working with him."

"Abby!"

"What?" she yells from her bedroom. "I said I don't have much advice for you, but I do know someone who might."

"If you say Maverick, I'm going to give you a thirty-second notice to move out."

"His name is Maverick? That's a freaking sexy name," she says, stepping back into the living room wearing a Black Alcove t-shirt.

"Abby …"

"All right, all right, Sara is stopping by the BA tonight. Come with me to work, we'll serve you a few drinks and talk about your problems, and then you can decide what to do. Sometimes a less-than-sober brain can make some pretty awesome decisions."

"I'm going to disagree with that, but a drink sounds pretty good. Just one though—I can't drink too much since I have to work tomorrow and impress a lot of people."

* * *

Three glasses of wine later, I believe I can do anything. Mainly, work with Maverick without any side effects of his hot body in the room next to me. I won't have any middle-of-the- day daydreams about him. I won't envision the way he looks with his shirt off or how his pants look slightly unbuttoned and hanging off his hips just right so you can see that amazing v dipping right to the perfect bulge of—

"Seriously, whatever you're thinking about or possibly drinking, I need some," Kelsey says, and she's practically blushing as she looks at Sara. Two of my best friends, *married* best friends, give each other a knowing look before focusing back on me.

"What's that look for?" I put a hand up. "No, wait, don't answer that. That is the exact look you two used to give each other when we would talk about Sky and Luke. Whatever you are thinking, stop. Stop right now."

"Well, we've all gone through the denial phase of falling for a guy, Beth."

"And yet your left ring fingers display how miserably you failed." I wave my hand up. "This bare thing waves nothing but success."

"It's only day one. That will change," Sara says.

Doubt it.

"It probably won't, considering she tried to bang him over the weekend and it didn't work out," Abby so kindly reveals as she drops off another round of drinks at the table.

"You're kidding." Kelsey gasps, her hand over her chest.

"Thank you, Abby, for sharing that," I say.

"Of course," she grins and walks off.

Every day. Every. Day. I ask myself why I am still friends with her. How is anyone in our group still friends with her?

"You can't just let her drop a bomb like that and not fill in the rest of the story," Sara says.

"Well ..." I take another drink. "That pretty much summed it up."

"No way. There is the who, what, when, where, and how," Kelsey adds.

"No, no, no, this is not another book idea," I say.

"Everything can be made into a book," Sara says.

"Yep," Kelsey agrees. "As long as the right person is writing it, it's true."

"Well, if this is opening an idea for you, I'm not sharing anything."

Their blank expressions surprise me. These two always have a comeback. Always.

When their silence continues, I crack. "What?"

"You are the bluntest person I know. You have never cared what we thought, yet something happened with this guy and now you're all … secrets," Sara says.

"You care what we think, so that means you care about him," Kelsey adds.

This time, *I* don't have anything to say. What in the heck have these two been smoking? Who comes up with this shit? Being blunt and sharing all my secrets are not the same thing.

"And I think that last line is my cue to leave," I say, scooting out of the booth.

"No, no," they both say.

"We never get to come out without the kids." Kelsey pushes out her bottom lip.

"Technically," I point to Sara's growing belly, "you brought the kids."

They laugh.

"If you two would stop birthing children, we could go out a lot more. If one of you isn't pregnant, the other one is."

I give them both a quick side hug as they are still seated. "I've got to get going. I don't want to be late for my second day, and right now, I can already tell waking up is going to be hard to do."

"You were always such a lightweight." Sara laughs as I head out the door.

"Show him who's boss," Kelsey chimes in behind her. As lame as her comment might be, she has a point. I went to school for this. I busted my ass and devoted my time.

I may have said I was going home to get to bed, but that's

a lie. I need something to bring with me to work in the morning. Something to show him how dedicated I am.

Tomorrow I am going to show Maverick that he isn't going to distract me and that I can do this pitch with or without him. Nothing he can do will stop me from earning this position.

Maverick

When I was younger, my mother used to tell me that I was the most headstrong little boy she knew. That I had more drive to accomplish things in life than most grown men she'd ever met. Aside from my father, of course.

Each time I came home from school with another A, another award, or a letter from the school explaining how I should be placed in advanced classes of some kind, she'd repeat those words to me. And each time she said them, I never wanted to let her down. I would do everything it took to be sure I was the man she always believed I was. I never did let her down, and now that she is gone, I've passed this feeling on to my father.

I came back to my temporary apartment tonight, the one my father found for me before I even knew I was coming here, to consider a few ideas I have for social media promotion for the station. That's our first task.

Everything came to a halt when I opened my email. The one from my father to Mark, the guy who despises me the most for landing more contracts, confirming him as my active replacement while I am out of the Rockland office.

I knew they'd have to continue my work without me, but a

part of me was allowing myself to believe I could have both my job and the recruitment. Looks like I can't.

I pull out my phone and let it ring longer than usual this time as I wait for my father to pick up the other end of the line. Either way, I want him to know that I am still available for anything he needs as his employee.

I tap the red button on my phone when the "Hi, you've reached me" message takes over and sit back on my brown leather couch.

I could always drive there this weekend. See how things are going. Find out if there is anything he needs me to do, even with my current status.

I wish I could say that status is under control, but I would be lying to myself.

Just because Beth is more beautiful than any other woman I've met before and in the same office I do, doesn't mean I have to be attracted to her. Then again, I met her beforehand, so I don't really know where this falls.

No, I do know. I'm just struggling to accept it.

I grab my phone and scroll though the contacts. I need a distraction. A drink with the guys would do that, but since I'm not from here, I only know a few people from my previous visits. Of, course they all work for the company or used to—some left on their own choice.

I come to Drew's name first and press send.

No answer.

Next up, Greg.

No answer.

I pass a few other names, most of whom I don't feel like calling. Mainly because a drink sounds good but drinking till I'm black-out drunk doesn't.

A name pops up that I honestly forgot was in my phone. Tyler Maron. I met him during the one semester I took a marketing class at Wind Valley College.

I press the green button and wait.

"Mav, it's been a while." There's a chuckle to his greeting. If I recall, the last time I saw Tyler, we were leaving campus and this blonde chick marched up to him and hit him with her backpack. Right after he finished shouting at her to stop, she began screaming at him over something that had to do with a friend or girl who used to be a friend or something along those lines. I just know she was pissed.

"I figured you needed a decent amount of time to take care of your lady drama," I say and somehow, the words immediately bring Beth to mind.

"Oh man, I will never forget that day, even if it was a couple years ago. I wish I could say any drama with that particular one is gone, but I fear she'll always be around."

I ask. "Care to meet for a drink and forget about it?"

He laughs more. "That is definitely something I can do. The BA in thirty?"

"The BA?"

"The Black Alcove bar. We went there once, I think, while you were here. It's down near the park square."

"Right, okay. I'll see you there," I agree and we hang up.

* * *

I push open the door to The Black Alcove and am instantly surprised at the number of people here on a Monday night. Being a college town—even during the summer months— probably has something to do with it.

I spot Tyler standing at the end of the bar. He's leaning forward in a similar black slacks and button-down shirt ensemble that I am wearing, talking to a woman who's balancing a small round tray on her hip. As I get closer, I recognize her as the same crazy girl from school that day.

"Hey man," I say, grabbing his attention.

"Mav." He shakes my hand. "It's good to have you back in town."

"It's good to be back." I nod and pull out a seat. He takes the one next to me.

"Abby, this is Maverick. Maverick, Abby."

We shake hands and I smile, but I don't miss the way her eyes narrow at me.

"Maverick, huh? That's not a very common name," she says.

"No, it's not. I actually don't know anyone else with the same name."

She smirks.

"Neither do I, yet for some reason, I feel like I know you already."

I start to speak, but her shout stalls me.

"Girls," she yells down the bar. The women, one blonde and one brunette, turn to look at her. "This is Ty's friend." A large smile stretches across her face. "His name is Maverick."

One jaw drops and a set of eyes go wide. Then they both break into a set of laughter.

"Abs, whatever you're doing, stop," Tyler says, and she rolls her eyes.

"You can wait for Luke or Sky to get your drinks."

"Abby, seriously?" he asks. She just walks away.

I feel really out of place.

"Is there a reason you wanted to pick this bar? It doesn't seem very relaxing," I say.

"It is. I just never know what kind of mood Abby's going to be in when she sees me. She was fine till you walked in. So thanks for that," he says with a slight chuckle.

Once we have beers, we wander over to the only empty pool table out of the four along the back wall. Very similar to the bar in CO.

"You ever been in love, Maverick?" Tyler asks then pulls a pool stick from its place against the wall.

Beth's face flashes to mind. I shake the thought and take a few gulps of my beer. "No. Not that I know of."

"Well, if you ever do, take it from me. Anything you have to give up or fight for or break or whatever, just do it. If you don't, you'll be where I am and stuck trying to win her back."

I glance back to the bar where Abby is watching us. Tyler takes the first shot, the pool cracking against the balls. After a while, he changes the conversation to sports, we drink two beers, and play three rounds of pool. By the end of the night, I walk out a hundred dollars richer and only slightly more confused on what I should do about Beth. Or if I should do anything at all.

CHAPTER FIVE

Beth

"Good morning," Ann greets me as I step off the elevator. My shoulders loosen as I take in her smile. If she greets me every morning with this perky of an attitude, it's going to be hard walking in here every day worrying over working with Maverick.

"Good morning," I reply with a wave as I head for my office.

It's not like I can't do my job just because he is in the room next me. It's just unfortunate that if I need to talk to anyone throughout the day about the project, he'll be the first person I go to. Because let's be honest, Austin is going to be no help. Maverick will not affect me. And I will repeat this every day until I accept its truth.

His evergreen smell reaches me before I've even stepped into my office.

Maverick is leaned back in my chair with his feet propped up on my desk. He's reading something and judging from his engrossed level, I gather he's been here for more than just a few minutes.

Just fucking great.

"Good morning, Maverick. Are you ready to get started?" I ask, keeping my tone completely professional when I really want to tell him to get his polished black shoes that look like they've never set foot outside off my clean desk. But that wouldn't really make sense, seeing as how they aren't dirty. But I'd do anything in the moment to get that sexy smirk off his face. And "anything" is not a good idea when a new vision of us naked on my desk just popped into my mind.

"Beth," he says, retuning his feet to the floor and adjusting his tie as he sits up. "How are you today?"

"Ready to work. Where's Austin? He was on the email I sent out asking you both to meet me in my office this morning." I'd sent the email with intentions of diving into work so I wouldn't be tempted to think of Maverick. It's clearly not working because I'm pretty certain we could both fit in that chair as long as I kept my knees bent.

"Are you always in such a serious work mode when you arrive?" he asks.

"From the moment I walk through those doors to the moment I leave, yes." Good. Glad he's focused.

"You're just saying that to impress me." He laughs.

"Nope. It's a real thing. Some of us are here because we want to be and because we worked hard to get here."

His brows dip and his mouth twitches between anger and disappointment. The tick in his jaw is a pretty good indicator that he didn't like what I just said.

"There are very few people on this floor, Ms. Moyer, who didn't earn their place here. I gather from your tone a moment ago that you believe I am one of those people, and I assure you, I am not."

I press my lips together, and when I have to take a deep breath to keep myself from apologizing like a crazy person or from spouting some smart-ass remark, my chest rises so dramatically, it draws his eyes.

Men.

"Believe it or not"—his eyes flicker to mine—"I enjoy this business and I think I'm really good at it."

I'll bet he's good at a lot of things. And I'd like to try a few of those things right now, but that would defeat my whole goal of not imagining Maverick naked today. Which has failed twice now. Fuck.

My body and brain act like the damn battery ran down and everything but the sex button has forgotten how to function properly around him.

"All right then, since Austin is late, let's get to work and we can catch him up when he gets here." Yes, okay. I'm charged back up. I point to another seat for Maverick and then take my own when he stands. I wiggle the mouse to wake up my computer as I say, "I did a little research last night, and from what I found, our radio company does the least amount of marketing of any radio station in town."

Maverick unbuttons his coat and takes a seat in one of the chairs across from me. With one ankle crossed over his knee, he says, "Well, that would make sense on why they hired us. They need more advertisement."

"*More* is the key word that doesn't even fit. You have to have a little to need more, and they have none. They need their name out there, period. Their website says it's invalid, probably the result of someone not renewing the domain name, and they don't even have a Facebook page. Everyone these days knows that, as awful as Facebook is, it is one of the best tools for a business."

I pull up the files I emailed myself last night after I got home from the bar. Sleep wasn't easy once I dove into researching the station. I twist my computer to show Maverick.

"This row represents all the different ways we could market the company," I point out. "And these columns are the leading radio stations in town. Each check mark applies to which types of advertising the companies use. If you notice, each one uses different ones and they only use about half the entire list. TACM could be the first to use 100 percent of the possibilities."

I nod as I finish my mini speech. I know I'm smiling, too. The idea of helping a company get recognized and grow their fan base gets my blood pumping. And this spreadsheet is only the beginning

Maverick doesn't say anything right away, and when I try to read his expression, I'm not sure what to make of what I see. He's focused on me and not the screen, and his mouth is tugged to the side with a smile. Happiness comes to mind, but the swirling feeling his gaze sends to my lower stomach makes me think this look means something else entirely.

"You really were meant for this job, weren't you?" he asks.

"Well, I didn't take full course loads and more during spring, summer, and fall semesters till I graduated for nothing. This is what I want to do. I, too, think I'm really good at it, even if this is my first job. I like how it makes me feel. It's exciting."

"I noticed." His words are deep as he leans forward. "I'm not so sure you'll—"

"Good morning."

We both jump at Austin's greeting as he steps into my office.

"Sorry, did I catch you at a bad time?" He asks the question loudly enough for the both of us, but the stern look in his eyes is set on Maverick.

"No, Beth was just showing me the spreadsheet she put together last night on the different opportunities we have to advertise this company," Maverick tells him.

Austin steps in close enough to get a look.

"Well done. It's almost as good as the one I put together last night."

"Really?" I ask. He did work? That surprises me, but it's awesome. "Can you forward it to me? We could compare and then make a game plan from there."

"Your list is already on the screen." He sighs and pulls out his phone. "I'm sure we can make one from that."

My guess is he didn't even do anything project related last night.

I chance a glance at Maverick, who is staring at Austin with a raised brow and annoyance written all over his face.

"The event center holds an annual Fourth of July fireworks show each year." Maverick dives right into work talk, ignoring Austin. "They'll need a radio station to host the event. This would be great exposure for TACM. I've already contacted the center and pitched the idea. I think we should go with a major social media target on this one."

"You pitched something for our client without us?" I ask. That's bullshit. I glance to Austin to see if he agrees, but he's focused on his phone. I move my glare to Maverick.

He tilts his head and shrugs. "I could have waited and there would have been a chance we'd miss our opportunity."

"You should have discussed it with me or"— " I look at Austin. Must be something damn good on his phone "— whoever before you made that decision."

"I made the correct judgment in my choice to contact them." Maverick's voice is smooth and confident.

"Yeah, it was a genius idea, Maverick, but Bart mentioned his appreciation for teamwork not even twenty-four hours ago. Don't you think you should show your respect to the way he runs his company and what he expects of his employees by putting in the effort he asked for?"

Maverick clears his throat and leans back, his eyes connecting with mine. "You are correct. My apologies. It won't happen again."

"Okay." Shit, now what do I say? I was on a roll and he agreed and now … okay … I got this.

"Do you want to put together a Facebook page for them? Send out some ads? If we want the event center to choose them, we need to get their name in front of as many people as possible."

"Yes, I'll have it by lunch," Maverick answers, and a giddy feeling fizzes in my gut. Despite him making a choice without me, it's obvious we want the same things for our client.

"Could we go over the page and campaign idea after lunch?" I ask him.

"Works for me," Maverick answers.

Well, these short answers are not my favorite.

"Yeah, not for me though," Austin says. I almost forgot he was there. "I have appointments all afternoon."

"Doing what?" Maverick asks.

"It doesn't concern you." Austin stands and heads for the door. Pretty sure his not being available for the team does, in fact, concern us.

"Tonight then?" I speak up. We have to work on this sometime, and if outside office hours is when he's available, I'll rearrange my schedule.

A grin that makes me shift in my seat and look away appears on Austin's face. "Sure," he says. "Seven o'clock? The steakhouse on Evans Street."

"Okay," I answer.

"This isn't on your time, Austin." Maverick's stern tone is thick. "Don't be late."

"Right," Austin says and is gone.

When Maverick turns back around, he gives me a sad attempt at a smile.

"I'll get to work on that page, then, and see you tonight."

I nod, watching him as he leaves. Working with these two is going to be a pain in my ass. Austin doesn't seem to want to help with anything, and Maverick … well … he distracts my mind from work both in the fact that he looks good—god, that scruff is sexy—and because seeking out a venue for the station to host on a fucking holiday was a goddamn brilliant idea and I should have thought of it first. Ugh, I want him even more knowing he's going to work just as hard on this as I am.

I've got this though.

I have to.

I need it.

Whatever it takes, I can do this.

* * *

The day passes quickly and I'm glad. Not meeting this afternoon to go over these first few steps of digital advertisement has cost us work hours. That's not something I enjoy.

I apply a gloss layer over my lips and grab my purse and coat before I head for the door. Coming back to my apartment for some downtime between work and this dinner meeting was a good idea up until the moment when I fought with myself to wear jeans instead of my work attire. The skirt and blouse won, again.

My cell buzzes inside my purse as I reach my car, and my brother's name appears on the screen.

"Hey, Phil," I greet him and turn the key.

"Beth, we need to talk," he says.

"Oh it's good to hear from you too," I say.

"It's about Mom." He ignores my sarcasm.

"Of course it is."

"Why aren't you answering her calls?"

"Um, for the same reason I never do. So I don't have to listen to her yell at me for moving to Wyoming with Dad as a kid. So I don't have to listen to her talk shit on Dad. So I don't—"

"Beth."

"What?" I haven't even pulled away from the curb. Whatever he is about to say, I assume I shouldn't be driving when I hear it.

"There's this job, in New York, and I think it would be

great for me," he says. He sounds hopeful, exactly like I used to about this marketing job.

"Okay, so what do you need to talk to me about?" I ask, even though I know. It's the same reason he came here right before Christmas. He wants me to move and take care of Mom, in Montana. He's been doing it for the last couple years. I know a good sister and a good daughter would drop everything to help family, but I just don't think it would do her any good. She needs more help than Phil or I can give her.

"Take my place at Mom's," he says.

"I can't."

"Why? Because you have to sacrifice part of your life? What do you think I've been doing? It's your turn, Beth."

"Phil, you chose to take that responsibility on your own. I didn't force you."

"She needs us. She needs her kids."

"No."

"Beth, please. I don't want her to go to some home. She misses you, and I'm almost convinced if you come home, things might change for her."

"I can't, Phil. Drop it." My eyes burn as I snap at him.

"Can't or won't?" he asks. The line falls silent as he waits for answer.

"I just got this new job. I can't leave now," I tell him.

"So they offered it to you?" he asks, and despite our current topic, he actually sounds happy for me.

"Not yet. But I know they will."

"And if they don't?"

"I don't know. Find another job."

"You're my baby sister, so I'll make you a deal. You get this job, I'll stay with Mom and we can consider a treatment facility for her. You don't get the job, you take my spot and if she's not improving after a year, we will reconsider our options."

A tear breaks free. I want Mom to get better. I really do.

After the divorce, Phil was always the best brother even if we lived miles away. If I don't get this job, the right thing would be to let him go for the one he wants. It's only fair, right?

"Okay," I tell him.

"Seriously?" Enough excitement to last a lifetime blares through the phone. "Beth, thank you! Thank you!"

His happiness overtakes him as he stutters a few more thanks you and then tells me he'll call me later.

It was good to hear from him even if it wasn't for the reason I would have wanted; I miss him and I know what he wants from me is reasonable.

But now I want this job at Mitchell Marketing more than anything.

Maverick

I arrive at the restaurant at a quarter till. I don't see either Beth or Austin, so I take a seat in the lounge. We aren't having dinner. This is a work meeting only.

I've barely sat down when Beth walks through the door. She's still in the skirt and jacket she had on earlier, looking radiant as ever. I smile and wave her over.

This is work, not a date, I remind myself one more time.

"Where's Austin?" she asks. I can't help but laugh. When it comes to work, she sure is serious. This kind of attitude would be very beneficial for the company.

"Does it surprise you that he isn't here yet?"

The waitress places water glasses on the table. "Can I get you anything else to drink?"

"Water is fine. We are waiting on one more," Beth answers. The waitress leaves us, and I can't help but smile.

"What?" Beth asks.

"You're like a lion ready to pounce."

"Well, I am here to work and I want to get started."

"It's okay to relax though. I mean, we are going to be working together for a while. Being comfortable around each other will help us process more smoothly."

"I'm comfortable."

"Are you sure?"

"Yes."

My brow raises. I'm not so sure.

She releases a big sigh.

"Fine, but how would you feel being in my position? Up against two family members of the company."

She has a point.

"Well, for starters, Austin isn't much to work against. He isn't even here," I tell her.

"But he's the boss's son. That already puts him in a higher place than me."

"I wouldn't assume that."

"Still, I can't be messing around. My life depends on this job."

A worried look that almost clashes with desperation flashes through her eyes. What would a woman right out of college have to fear? Money? This could be an interesting topic to explore, but my damn phone picks right now to ring.

"It's Austin," I say before answering it.

"Are you almost here?" I ask.

"No."

"What do you mean, no?"

Beth's eyes go wide.

"I relocated the meeting. Meet me at the corner of Stone and Fifth."

"Stone and Fifth," I say out loud. Beth pulls out her phone and types in the address. Her brows furrow as she holds the phone closer to her face.

"It's a strip club," she mouths.

"Austin, come on, we can't meet there."

"Scared of the temptation?" he asks.

"I don't even know what that means." Seriously, what the fuck does that mean?

Beth taps her finger on the table in front of me. "Let's just go and get this over with."

"Fine," I say to both her and Austin. "We are on our way."

The last place most women want to be is in a strip club, yet Beth accepted the idea like I was asking her if she wanted to grab a drink. I've heard of people doing what it takes to get a job, but her drive has got to be on a whole different level.

"Austin doesn't play fair. I'm warning you now. Let's just cut him from the team. He can work on his own," I offer.

"Cut the boss's son? How do you think that will make us look?" She acts like I've just said the craziest thing in the world to her.

"You don't know him like I do."

"Suck it up, Maverick. Don't be a baby."

"I'm not being a baby. I'm looking out for you."

"I don't need you to look out for me."

She marches out of the restaurant and straight for her car.

Looks like we're doing this. She rolls down her window and yells for me to get into her passenger's seat.

"Nothing about this is a good idea, but if you think we should go, we will go," I say.

"Thank you."

"However, I would like to point out that he made this work decision without us, so feel free to call him out on it."

If she's going to call me out on my bullshit, she should do the same to him. Although her ability to put me in my place earlier turned me on more than it upset me, so I definitely don't hope for the same reaction when it comes to Austin. Plus, perhaps my comment will get a slight rise out of her. Her cheeks turn this glowing shade of pink when she's upset and a dimple appears on the left side of her mouth when she presses her lips together so she doesn't say the wrong thing. It's only been a couple of days, but she does this more than you'd think.

"Hey, I expect this behavior from him, not you," she says.

"You're right."

"Exactly."

I steal a glance and catch the smile she's attempting to hide with her hand.

"You can't always be right, though," I tempt her.

"Ah, we'll see."

When we pull up to the club, it looks run down and in need of paint. Something I'm sure most people would never notice coming here at night, but since there is still a sliver of daylight, this place gives the illusion that it's deserted instead of a business.

"We will just get in, get out and be on our way," Beth says, her steps faltering as she approaches the door.

"Having your doubts now?" I ask.

"No, I just would rather not spend my entire night in a hazy strip club."

"Agreed," I say, and we step inside.

Smoke engulfs us the moment we step inside and Beth immediately starts coughing. The urge to tell her to wait outside so she doesn't have to endure this hits me, but before I can say anything, she walking farther inside.

Fucking Austin. I should have known he would pull this shit. I grip the back of my neck as I make way behind Beth. He is up to something, and I don't think it's going to end well for any of us.

Beth spots him before I do. She takes a seat at his table, pulling out a notepad and pen.

"You have all your fancy spreadsheets written down on there?" Austin asks, his eyes never leaving the woman on stage.

"Well, I sure as shit am not going to bring a laptop in here."

"Why not? Think you're better than the women in here?"

"Austin," I warn.

"Let's just get to work," Beth says.

"On one condition," Austin says, and I cross my arms. Now were going to find out exactly why he wanted us to come here.

"You dance and then we can work."

"Are you fucking kidding me?" I shout as Beth gasps.

"That's insane," she snaps. "For fuck's sake, how mental are you?"

"Mental enough to know you want this job this badly.

Mental enough to know you'd rather work on this project without me. And I'll give you that, if you dance."

Beth leans back in her chair, her focus locked on Austin. Her tongue sweeps across her lips right before her teeth tug against the bottom one.

This is not the place for me to begin thinking about how that should be my tongue and my lips.

"No, no, don't even think about it, Beth. He's setting you up," I say. She's still focused on him.

"She's a big girl; she can make her own choice."

"Beth, come on, he's just trying to see how far he can get you to go. It's not worth it." Her eyes finally flicker to me briefly before returning to Austin.

"I'm not dancing for anyone," she answers.

Thank god.

"Of course not. Mav wouldn't be able to contain himself if you did," Austin says.

Big, green eyes focus on me.

"What's that supposed to mean?" she asks, probably assuming I shared information about this past weekend.

"Oh, he didn't tell you why he's at MM under my father's watch and not with his own?"

"Austin, just get to it so Beth and I can get on with our work," I interrupt.

His eyes narrow as he looks me up and down. "Keeping it a secret? Fine. You dance for him, really dance for him to the next song, and I'll let you two be."

Dance for me? I thought it was dance in general. I rub my hands over my face. How in the fuck did my serious career bring me to this moment? This has got to be a nightmare. This isn't real.

"I already told you, no."

"Just one dance," he says.

Fuck. This is not a dream and this isn't good.

Beth's eyes flash to the stage.

"I want him gone, too, but this? This is not the way to do it," I tell her.

"You think I don't know that?" she snaps.

She jumps from her seat and grabs her bag, shoving her notepad inside.

"Fuck off, Austin."

I'm ready to knock him out when he doesn't even look at her to say, "It's your future, not mine. No dance means I'll go ahead and let the two of you take the reins, but my name will be included in everything. Let me know when you need me."

Rolling her eyes, Beth beelines it for the door.

"Beth," I call out behind her.

"Don't, Maverick."

"Hey, I just want to make sure you're okay."

I really wish I knew what she was thinking in there. She acts tough, but I can see that this was too much on her. I could see that she almost agreed to dance for Austin … for a job.

"I'm fine. I don't want to talk about it."

We climb inside her car once more, and when we get back to the restaurant it's hard to miss her shaking hands as she puts the car in park.

"We'll both have three ideas for Facebook advertising by morning, yeah?" she asks. "Maybe for something else, too." She shakes her head and looks forward. "Just anything, really."

"Beth—"

"What's done is done, Maverick. If my choice ruins my

chance of a job, fine, I don't want to earn it that way anyway. I'll see you in the morning," she cuts me off.

I nod, wishing there was something I could say to her. Austin is on a whole different level with his determination to get this job. I have a to find a way to make it easier for Beth. Running off to tell on Austin isn't in the cards. With my background, I don't his father, or mine, would believe me at this point. I've got to think of something. In the meantime, doing exactly as she asks is a great place to start.

CHAPTER SIX

Maverick

What the fuck am I doing?

I told Beth I would have something for her today, but I haven't done anything. The most I've accomplished since last night was obtaining a photo of TACM's current logo and sending it over to the design team to see if there was any way they could make it more modern, more hip, and a lot less cartoonish. TACM has been around since before I was born and, although we still want to keep the family-friendly vibe the station has, it is time for a new look.

It hasn't even been twelve hours since I last saw her and I can't force myself to think of anything but her. I can't do this. I can't let my job slip. I can't be flirting with her. I shouldn't even allow myself to be eager to see her the way I am this morning. She is my coworker. How in the hell did I let the line blur after just a few days? President of MM has been my goal since high school since I saw how a product of any kind, when marketed well, could bring a family together. This is the job for me. I just need to remind my brain of that.

Beth emailed me this morning to see if we could get together to go over some of her ideas. I'm guessing she hopes that I'll go over some of the points I have as well, but I've got nothing. Zilch. Nada. *Brain, you can start functioning appropriately any time now.*

The only thing I've got is a reason why I can't fool around with Beth.

We work together and I need my job back. Which means we can't. I'm a mix between frustration and annoyance that this one woman can soak up so much of my time. Work has always been my top priority. I've never thought about someone as much I have thought about Beth. I may have figured out the reason, too. We haven't had sex. If we'd just have sex, I'd be able to stop thinking her. Piece of cake. Then again, shit, sex is what got me here in the first place.

"Maverick?"

"Yeah," I say, jumping as Beth pokes her head inside my office.

"Are you okay? You look a little flushed and you have all your blinds closed."

"No, yeah, I'm fine. Just have a lot on my mind right now."

She nods. "I can understand that."

Her hair is straight today, and it isn't until this moment that I realize how long it is and how sleek it looks down the middle of her back. She's wearing a black dress that falls to just below her knees, with a slit up the left side. The same side that is also revealing enough leg to show me the definition of her slender thigh all the way down to the matching heels. This dress displays exactly how amazing her body is, and the gold shiny belt she has is so loose around her waist, she might as well get rid of it. I could help her do that.

"Maverick, is now a bad time?"

"Bad time for what?" I ask, snapping out of whatever the hell world I just went to obsessing over her clothes. I still prefer no clothes, but—

"Maverick?"

"Huh?"

Shit. I have got to pay attention.

"I'll come back. It's fine."

"No, no, let's work on it now."

She smiles like I've made her day.

"All right, can you pull up the new spreadsheet I sent you?"

I do as she asks and listen as she speaks about numbers. How can she be so focused at work? Am I imagining every little pull of attraction between us? Maybe I am the only one who feels this way.

"And then right here …" She moves in closer to show me what she's talking about. I think it's obvious my attention right now is lacking. "This is where we can make our first slide. It can be a glimpse of the future, and this …" She points again, but this time she leans a little too far and neither of us misses the second her breast brushes up against my bicep. I sure as hell don't miss the part where she stops moving and leaves it there. I try not to think about it but fail miserably when I look up to find her watching me. The moment her tongue slips out to lick her lips, all control is lost.

In a matter of seconds, my chair is bouncing off the back wall as my body presses her against the desk. She drops her pen and turns to face me. The touch of her fingers as they curl my shirt at the sides is all I need to know she feels the same way I do.

"Maverick," she whispers. I tilt her chin up, forcing her to look to me. Her eyes search mine, begging for me to come up with a reason why we shouldn't do this. I can't think of a single excuse.

I capture her lips against mine, slow and gentle at first. They brush once, twice, over hers before she jerks me against her and slides her tongue over my lips, deepening the kiss. Without breaking the seal, I glide my hands under her thighs and lift her onto my desk. Her legs part to let me step between them, and thank god for that damn slit allowing just enough room.

Beth's hands slide from my sides to my back and down over my ass. She gives me a tug, but I don't let our bodies connect. I leave enough room between us to allow one hand to caress her inner thigh. The exact way I was last night.

Her head falls back at my touch. I kiss her neck, her chest, and move the top of her dress aside just enough to tease her. All while my hand sneaks closer and closer to the spot where I want to be most.

"Maverick, this is the worst idea."

"I know," I agree, but we don't stop. When our eyes lock, I slide her panties to the side and slip a finger inside her.

"Maverick," she pants as I—

"Hey, open the door." Austin knocks loudly. My hand jerks back and Beth shoves me away from her.

"Fuck," I say.

"Shit," she says and we both stare at the door like it's going to open on its own.

I catch the shadow that moves by my window toward Beth's office door.

"He's going to go through your office," I tell her.

She looks at me with wide, panicked eyes. Right before Austin steps through her door into my office, Beth sits in a chair across from my desk, I take a seat behind my desk and I turn my computer to face her.

"Yes, and I think we should do that before anything else," Beth says, her voice scarily, completely back in her work tone.

"Why is your door locked?" Austin asks, narrow eyes glancing back and forth between Beth and me. His hands are at his hips by the time he settles his gaze on me.

"We're working, Austin. We get more done when we don't have any distractions." I point to him, hoping he'll understand what I mean.

"Oh, of course, I won't stay long."

"Great," I say. I'm not leaving room for more conversation.

"I mean, you really don't need any more distractions than you have already," he says. Then he moves his gaze to Beth. "Oh, yeah and be sure to ask Mav why he's here. We never really got to cover it last night."

"I'll keep that in mind," she replies, her gaze meeting mine just briefly. "After we start with our introduction, I think should keep the feel more positive and focus on what TACM can be doing instead of what they haven't done."

"I agree," I say and smile at Austin. "Is there anything else?"

His eyes narrow once more before he turns for my door. He leaves the door both unlocked and open when he leaves.

I chuckle a bit before returning to the discussion of our presentation.

"This isn't funny, Maverick."

I love how she still calls me by my full name. Only she could make it sound so seductive.

"It kind of is,' I say.

Her brow peaks and I nod.

"You're right. It's not funny."

"That can't happen again," she tells me, but even as she says it, I don't think even she believes her own words.

Almost immediately, it's like every person on the floor has to walk by my office, their eyes meeting mine. The last man, whose name I don't know, nearly breaks his neck while peering past my door.

It's like they are all waiting for me to fail. To be the guy they probably heard I was.

Aside from the fact I just broke my father's number one rule and that, if reported, would reflect on the final decision to promote me, Beth's chances of making it here after ninety days will be stronger if people don't know there's anything between us.

Which should be easy, because there isn't.

"Again, you're absolutely right." I keep my eyes focused on the computer in front of me as I swivel it back around. "I'll review this and send you an email. I'm sure most of what we want to accomplish today can be done with you in your office and me in mine."

"Maverick, I didn't mean it like that. I just meant—"

"Either way, I'm not offended, but I do think it's for the best."

"Sure, *Mav*. Of course," she replies, her tone dry and that pink color taking over her cheeks.

"Would you mind closing my door?" I ask just as she is stepping into her own space.

Ah, she must not have heard me.

When she's gone, I lean back in my chair and let out a sigh. If anyone knew what I was thinking right now, they would recognize every ounce of frustration this sigh represents. I finally meet a woman I can't stop thinking about and she's off limits.

I'm resisting every urge I have right now to start making my own rules.

Somehow, no matter what I decide to do, I have the feeling I'm still making all the wrong choices.

Beth

What a fucking ass. I mean seriously, what a *jackass*. I drop the spiral notebook onto my desk and groan as I take my seat. *Oh, hey, let me get you all worked up and then get mad because I don't know what I want.* I guarantee that's his thought process right now. I may be conflicted with this entire situation, but shit, at least I was going to suggest we try to keep anything like that from happening at the office. Just the office. But I didn't even get that far before his panties got twisted into a bunch and he threw me out. I felt like a child who mouthed off to her father and was sent back to my room. Thanks, Dad. God. Such a jackass.

I take a deep breath and let it out slowly. All right, I'm done being mad. I have work to do. Since my damn computer is on a ten-second timer to fall asleep, I wake it once again to pick up where I left off before I went to Maverick's office. I open a new search bar on the Internet to search local businesses that might be interested in supporting the station when a little box pops up in the lower right-hand side of my computer screen.

"Message from Mav …"

It's actually a cool nickname.

No, he doesn't get a nickname. He doesn't get anything.

For reasons I'm unsure of, I check my doorway and the open windows of my office. Not a single person is aware of what I'm doing.

I open the message box.

Mav: I'm sorry.

Beth: For?

Mav: You know.

Beth: It could be a number of things, really. I'll need you to be more specific.

Mav: I'm sorry for kicking you out the way I did.

Beth: Oh. All right.

Mav: I'm sorry because we work together and that can't happen again. But, trust me when I say, I'll never be sorry for kissing you, Beth.

My fingers hover over the keyboard as I contemplate my response.

That's good. Now stop acting like a child.

Of course, don't be silly.

I know.

Or my most favorite but most inappropriate: *Screw work. Let's do it again.*

Instead of any of those, I settle for the more mature route. Since I'm at work and all.

Beth: Thank you for apologizing.

A blurb in a tiny message under the textbox displays *Mav is typing ...*

I should get back to work and not sit here staring at the screen, waiting for his response. The message goes away and then pops back up, but still no response. I minimize the screen.

This is crazy. I don't think about guys like this. Ever. Nothing should change because of this one. How many times am I going to have to remind myself of this? There are way too many factors that could make this a messy situation. I can't afford to not get this job. A bad breakup would be the best-case scenario. If we dated. Which we aren't. So, I should just get back to work.

An hour later and I still can't stop my eyes from glancing at the message box at the bottom of my screen. The one not flashing with a reply. The one I should probably just exit out of all together so I can get my mind to focus. How in the fuck does anyone in a relationship get crap done? I can't get my brain to function after just a kiss.

As if my body now knows when he's near, I look up to see Mav passing my office. He doesn't glance over. My heart sinks.

It sinks even more with the realization that I've already let myself develop feelings for him. The one thing I've fought for so many years to do when it comes to men and Mav shows up and changes everything.

Maverick. Argh. He doesn't get a stupid nickname from me.

* * *

Skylar pours me another beer and sets it in front of me. This week has been killer. I'm so glad it's Friday. Working with Maverick after that kiss was … mentally exhausting.

"Do you want to talk about it?" she asks, folding her arms as she leans on the bar.

I shake my head.

My phone rings on the bar top next to my beer. My mother's face flashes across the screen. I tap the red button and then gulp back half my drink.

"Want to talk about *that*?" Sky glances to my phone before meeting my eyes.

Again, I shake my head.

How did I get so lucky that both my family and my work can stress me out? Aren't your home life and work life supposed to be the happiest places in life?

"I don't want this to come out as I'm an expert, but if anyone knows anything about wanting to escape and avoid all family, I'd probably be the best person for you to talk to."

I glance up see to a pair of concerned eyes and a soft smile.

"I just can't be the person my mom wants me to be. I'm always letting her down. She wants me to hate my father just as much as she does, and I know he hurt her, but it doesn't work like that. He's still my dad; he never stopped caring about me. And even if I do move to take care of her, I know it won't get better."

If I don't get this job, addressing these subjects will be like dragging a rusty nail over my skin. I really would rather not do it.

"She just doesn't want to feel alone," Sky says.

"She wouldn't be alone if she could let it go and stop drinking. If she could not talk about my dad's new girlfriend each time I saw her. I can't even remember the last time she asked me about my own life."

"Do you ask about hers?" Sky asks.

My brow peaks. "I don't exactly get a chance when she's blabbering on and on about my father and slurring her words so badly I can only make out the foul ones."

"She cares and has a bigger heart than a lot of moms out there. Just try changing the subject next time and maybe get her coffee or something. I don't really know that area."

Sky smiles at the man who just walked up beside my barstool. He orders a Bud Light and she hands him a bottle before bringing her attention back to me.

"I'm sorry Sky, here I am complaining because my mom calls me too much when—"

"When my mom hasn't called me since the day I left home. It's okay." She winks at me. "Just make it better. Don't give up on her."

I've spent more than enough nights with Sky as she's sobbed until she falls asleep over the fact her mother doesn't approve of her life here in Wind Valley. I don't ever want to be that way with my own mother, but it's been years since I felt my mom cared about anything other than what my father was doing without her. I wish I could say I believe she will move on and we can have a relationship again, but I don't think she ever will.

"Maverick kissed me this week," I blurt out, changing the subject.

Sky gives me a huge grin. "And?"

"And then he apologized and said it couldn't happen again."

"Ouch."

"You know why he did that though, don't you?" Luke, Sky's boyfriend, speaks up next to her.

"How long have you been listening to us?" she asks him, her hands on her hips. She's smiling, so it's clear she isn't mad.

"Longer than I should have," he answers her, following up his words with a kiss. "But you do know, don't you?" He looks at me.

I shrug with a small shake of my head. If I knew, I wouldn't be sitting here right now. I'd be working. Focusing. Being successful and not conflicted about the choices I've made lately.

Ugh. And all over a guy.

I finish off my drink and push it toward Sky.

"More, please."

She eyes me for a moment before handing me my refill.

"He said that because if you know it can't happen again, that makes two minds who know it shouldn't happen."

I wait for him to go on, but he doesn't.

"Real solid advice, Luke. I'm not sure how your wit landed you this woman," I say.

He doesn't deserve the attitude that came with that

remark, but I'm not sure how to have any other tone at the moment.

"Whoa, I'm not finished," he says. "If you both know, then when it does happen again, because it will, he won't be the only one at fault. He'll say he tried to warn you. That you could have stopped him and so on."

"So, you're saying he lied?" Sky asks.

"In a way, yeah, I guess."

"Well," I say and take a quick sip of my beer. "Not only is that the stupidest thing I've ever heard, but it sounds like a game I'm not interested in."

I pull cash from my purse and lay it between us.

"Thanks for the talk," I say and head home.

Moping isn't going to get me anywhere; I need to get my act together fast. My life depends on it, my job depends on it, and now, my heart does.

Maverick Mitchell will no longer be a problem for me, and the next time I see him, I'm going to let him know just that.

CHAPTER SEVEN

Beth

I really wish the confidence that came with a buzz would follow me to work in the mornings. I understand that Maverick is trying to be the good guy here and not fool around with someone he works with, but he's going to have to stop arriving to work in his perfect suit with his perfect hair and that perfect smile surrounded by that perfectly groomed face. It's been more than a week and everything about him still screams irresistible, and unfortunately—or fortunately, depending on how you look at it—my body hasn't yet learned what self-control is.

I also, obsessively, won't let this go.

"Hey, Maverick," I say, peeking into his office the way I always do when a quick message back and forth won't work. Especially since this time around, I'm not here for work. Nope, I'm basically walking into his office with full intentions of being up to no good. Just because he says this thing between us can't happen doesn't mean the conversation ends there. I get a say too, damn it.

"Good morning, Beth." He smiles at me from his desk. When I know I have his full attention I step through the doorway.

"I have a new print-out of the first slide," I say, my diversion for getting close to him.

"Great, I was actually thinking we should have a presentation with words and one without. The one with we could send to them, and the one without can be the one we present to them. That way they are actually listening to us and not reading the projection instead."

"That's a great idea." His enthusiasm only makes me want to make my next move more.

"Look, Maverick, I'm just going to get right to the point."

"Is everything okay?" he asks, standing as he watches me with concern.

"Yes, but I can't stop thinking about kissing you, and I was also thinking that maybe if we had sex once, I could get you out of my system and I'd be all set." The words are barely out of my mouth before he's capturing mine with his own.

Everything about our embrace right now is desperate. Hands moving feverishly from our hair to our hips to our asses, gripping or groping where we can as our bodies rub against each other.

I push him back on his chair, resting my knee between his legs as I lean over him, never breaking the kiss. His hands go straight to my butt. That's how far we get when I remember where we are. And that his door is wide open. And that's exactly where his hands are continuing to rest when we hear him.

"I'm just going to speak with Maverick for a quick second."

We both freeze at the sound of his uncle's voice.

"Hide, now, under the desk." Maverick nudges me; all the while I am protesting.

"You're joking, right?" I laugh at him. "Just hold it together."

"Uncle Bart, what can I do for you?"

I want to whisper that he shouldn't sound so eager, but I think that would defeat the purpose of the issue we're trying to hide right now. I don't think I've ever seen Maverick sweat like he is right now. He clearly doesn't seem to do well under pressure.

"Oh perfect, I was hoping to speak with you and Miss Moyer for a quick moment."

"Oh … yeah …" Maverick's choice of words trail off as he struggles to come up with something. Really, Maverick?

"About what, sir?" I ask and side glance Maverick. What the fuck is his deal?

"The owner of TACM contacted to me to let me know you pitched the station to the event center and that they accepted. He's quite pleased and so am I. I'd like to meet with you both in my office a bit later to go over more details."

"Of course," I answer him because Maverick apparently isn't talking anymore.

"Splendid, I'll have Ann send you an email with a time slot." He looks to Maverick. "Are you feeling okay?"

"Swell," he manages to squeak out.

"All right then, I'll see you both soon."

The moment he's out of view I swat Maverick's arm. "What the hell was that?"

"I'm not really sure, but I think you should go back to your office."

"What?"

"I have things to work on."

"Maverick, we have things to work on together."

"Just go." His voice is thick and I'm a little taken back. "Please."

"Fine, if that's how you want it." I grab the printed slides off his desk. "Strictly work it is." I head for my office.

"Beth, I just need a few minutes."

I pause and turn. "Trust me, Maverick, you can have all the time you need."

Maverick

It's after lunch by the time Beth and I meet in my uncle's office. I know she is irritated with me, but I'm even more frustrated with myself. I'm here for one reason and I can't even get my shit together long enough to get it done.

I feel extremely out of my element here, like I'm in high school all over again. Trying to get the girl by impressing her and doing the right thing. When I worked at the Colorado office, I felt much older than my twenty-six years; business is serious around there. It's not a group of people competing for a job. It is the job and it came with a lot more responsibility than the spot I'm in now. Back home, I was busy the entire workday overseeing multiple accounts; now I'm working on one and feel like I'm not doing anything all. Either this place needs more structure and more clients or being near Beth is throwing off my game.

I glance over at her, since we are both seated across from

my uncle, who is finishing up an email. She isn't looking at me and my uncle hasn't said a word. I'd say both the structure and the girl are what's wrong with me.

"So, I hear the two of you have decided to team up away from Austin," he says, folding his hands in front of him. He settles his eyes on Beth for a moment as she just nods and then he looks to me.

"Well, then, how's it going?"

"As good as can be expected," I answer.

"Yes," Beth agrees. "We still separated out some of the Fourth of July fireworks event duties, so in a way we are all still working together."

"That's good to hear. These next couple of weeks leading to the event will pass quickly."

"Yes, sir. Maverick and I have already contacted a few different companies who are willing to make donations for raffles during the event," she says. "Most of them are the same food and shop vendors that will be set up during the show. It's a great way to cross promote."

"They've agreed to work solely with TACM on their donations, too. The exclusivity will bring more people directly to us," I add.

"Good, good, this is what I like to hear." His computer pings. "I believe it's time for my next meeting. I'll schedule another meeting next week to go over your entire vision for the event."

"Of course."

He nods, and Beth and I file out of his office.

"Almost feels like sitting in the principal's office, doesn't it?" I ask.

Beth glares at me and turns for her office.

"Are you going to be mad at me forever or just today? I mean, we do have to work together and all."

"I'll talk when it's necessary, and your poor attempt at a joke is not a reason to talk to you."

"All righty then, when you're ready to talk, I'll fill you in on the progress I've made," I say.

"Or you can come to me when you have something because we are adults and not kids. I believe your 'come to me; no, go away; no, come back' vision of life is the exact definition of a child."

It impresses me that she speaks to me like she is my boss. Turns me on, too. I really do enjoy when she calls me out on this crap.

"I think I'll wait till you come to me," I say and walk past her.

I hear her huff as I turn the corner. She won't hold out long. We have a lot to do to be ready for the event.

CHAPTER EIGHT

Beth

I thought I'd be able to get more work done at home, without Maverick around, but my laptop is open and a bright white PowerPoint document stares back at me. Microsoft should have "Stop procrastinating and get to work already" appear on the screen to get people motivated. Then again, I know exactly what I need to be doing right now and I'm still not making any progress. And why am I not typing away and creating a marketing proposal on paper yet? Oh, because my idiotic partner on the project is holding out on his half until I talk to him. Without his research on TACM, I have only part of a plan. A half-assed proposal isn't going to keep me around after ninety days. I should go talk to Maverick, I know. But then he'll know he holds the cards, and I can't have that.

My purse buzzes on the kitchen counter behind me. Not only do we have the event to focus on right now, but we have a proposal to put together that will be presented to the client at the end of our ninety days. I refuse to move out of this seat until I have a least one more slide done. Preferably, the part that explains the outcome we'd like to receive from the said proposal *I'm* working on. I'll start with the end goal, and from there I can lay out the steps to make it happen. That part I know without Maverick being here.

My fingers finally start to glide over the keyboard when my phone buzzes again. I continue to ignore it, pressing my eyelids together to regain my focus.

What is Maverick's deal anyway? And I can't even run off to complain about him. I mean, I could, but considering I'm an adult now, I'm positive telling on him to his uncle isn't going to make me stand out. Well, not in the way I would like to stand out anyway.

A groan slips past my lips the moment my phone goes off for the fourth time in twenty minutes. Seriously, no one in this town needs my attention this badly. The legs on my chair don't scoot easily, and once I'm standing, my seat falls on its back with a loud thud. It hits the floor right before someone knocks on my door. Both loud noises cause me to jump.

What in the hell is going on?

Ignoring my phone, I answer my door instead.

"Hey." A coy grin greets me as Maverick leans against the frame. "I've been trying to call you," he says. I let the door slam closed in his face.

All right, so the end goal on this project should be to gain—

"Beth, come on, open the door."

I take a deep breath, release it slowly, and flip my chair upright.

So, the end goal should be to gain—

"Beth … come on."

… Should be to gain—

"Beth," he calls out my name again, just the way my phone kept going off before he showed up. If him standing outside my door is anything like his phone calls, I may as well get this over with and send him on his way.

"What?" I snap, jerking the door back open.

"You know"—he brushes past me as he enters my apartment, his minty scent taking over the air in front of me—"I can't say the attitude doesn't turn me on. Everything about you, actually, turns me on. It has since the first day we—"

"Why are you here and how in the hell do you know where I live?"

"I looked you up on the company website," he says like it's no big deal.

"They don't keep my address on there," I reply. I know because I've viewed the site before.

He chuckles and it sparks something inside me.

Dammit.

"I have connections."

I cross my arms, deciding against closing my door, because I don't plan for him to stay long. "I'm pretty sure there is a rule somewhere in that harassment pamphlet they gave me that says you can't do that."

"Did you read the entire booklet?" His head tips and he grins while he waits for my answer.

I hesitate. Of course I didn't read the whole thing. Harassment is common sense. "No, I didn't."

"I'm also pretty sure we've already broken most of the rules anyway," he adds. The click of his tongue against the back of his teeth redirects my attention to the mess of papers surrounding my computer on the kitchen table. That tongue has many talents. Just thinking about it makes me want to forget everything and shove him back onto my couch so I can shed his clothes and climb on top him. Finally bringing us to that point we've both craved. Maybe if we just have sex, he won't be so irresistible anymore.

Whoa. Shit. No. What am I thinking? I'm not some horny teenage boy. I'm a lady. And fuck if I don't have rules to stick to.

"Beth, did you hear me?" Maverick asks, and I don't miss the soft gaze in his eyes as he begins to take a step toward me.

Of course I didn't hear you. I was too busy imagining a way to get you naked. "Yeah," is how I answer, and from the satisfied look on his face, I'd say that was not the best answer to go with.

"Cool, I'll just be downstairs waiting then."

"Waiting for what?" I ask as he passes by me once again. For real, his smell alone can quicken my pulse.

Fuck. I have got to get a grip on this.

"To go to dinner and drinks? You know, what you just said yes to?"

"Oh no." I shake my head and take my seat at the table, twisting in my chair to look back at him. "I have work to do, but you do whatever you want."

I turn back around and pretend to be working, because let's face it, that control I wish I had isn't just going to magically appear. He doesn't say anything, and for a moment I think he left, deciding to give up, but when I turn around, my eyes meet his dark stare.

"If I could do whatever I want, I definitely wouldn't be standing here right now and you wouldn't be sitting at that table."

I try to hide the deep breath I inhale and release slowly. Pinching my lips together and looking up at him, I notice the way his eyes practically eat me up and his chest rises and falls quickly. I use every ounce of control I have not to jump across this table.

"I see you are back to your come-hither part of our relationship." I have to keep myself from laughing at my own comment. Laughter mean happiness and happiness means I enjoy his company. I'm still undecided, but leaning toward no.

"If you keep licking your lips the way you are right now, all rules against a workplace romance will be off the table … along with everything you have on it right now when I replace it with you lying on your back and me between your legs."

My chair flips over, again, as I stand. "Dinner sounds great. We should leave. Right now."

I'm doing this for myself so I can focus. Not for him.

"I'm only going because we work together and our lack of communication isn't good for this project."

"I couldn't agree more."

I brush past him with intent, the exact way he did earlier when he arrived, and I grab my jacket. With my purse over my shoulder and the last button on my coat fastened, I wave for him to exit first, ignoring the pleased look on his face.

I'd most likely enjoy just slamming the door behind him, locking him out, but just like before, I don't think he would leave. And right now is not the best time for me to test my self-control alone with him in my apartment. What he just said he would do is exactly what I want him to do to me.

Maverick chuckles, rubbing his facial hair and licking his lips as he walks in front of me. My head drops back and I close my eyes instead of looking at the ceiling.

With one more deep breath, I'm following him down the stairs. Just a quick trip out for dinner. How bad could it be?

Maverick

"Just one more shot."

"No. There is no way I can drink anymore," she says.

Her tongue occasionally darts out to glide over her lips as she speaks, leaving a glistening coat. I want to press my lips against hers just to have the taste of her mouth against my own. It's been only about a week since I last kissed her, but it feels like years. And both amounts of time are way too damn long.

Of course, I didn't plan to take her to dinner and get her drunk, but she's opening up a lot more than I expected her to, and that's beginning to be a problem for me. Tonight was supposed to be for me to get her out of my system. The night isn't even over yet and there is no doubt in my mind that my idea of hanging out with her to confirm there is nothing special about her is a complete backfire.

"Another round?" the blond bartender, I think her name is Sky, asks.

"No, no," Beth shakes her head with wide eyes.

"Just the check is all," I say, never taking my eyes off the beautiful redhead across from me.

She laughs and takes another sip of her drink. When her lips pull away from her straw, her cheeks grow an even brighter shade of red.

"Maverick, you can't keep looking at me like that."

"Like what?"

"Like a coworker should never look at a coworker. I mean, am I even wearing clothes in your eyes?"

I pause before I answer. Beth speaks her mind. She doesn't do much of the whole "think before you speak thing," and I like it. She's the most real person I've spoken to in years. People in this world have grown sensitive to almost everything around them. They're always afraid of hurting someone's feelings with the truth. If more people adopted Beth's approach, maybe they would realize that hiding the truth hurts more than revealing it. Then again, Beth and I haven't had a conversation tonight that would even remotely come close to hurting feelings. We've talked about beer, dinner, music, and she's filled me in on the lives of all her friends who work here.

"Maverick, stop." She laughs again, bringing me back into this moment with her.

"I can't help it."

"Here we go, back to the cheesy lines." Her eyes roll, landing on something toward the bar. I follow her gaze and catch sight of Sky and a guy whom I think is Luke behind the bar. He's got his arms locked behind her back while they kiss. People start shouting, but they continue to kiss for another ten seconds at least before Sky pulls away.

When I look back at Beth, she's still focused on them. She's smiling, but it doesn't stretch ear to ear. It reminds me of those smiles you see in movies, where the person is happy for what they see in front of them but sad because they wish they had it.

Beth has never come off as the type of woman who wants that type of relationship. Then again, I hardly know her, so I guess I wouldn't know what kind of relationship she really wants. Other than a one-night stand, which, according to her, is in the past and never happening again.

"Those two seem to make being a couple and working together look easy," I say.

"Maverick …"

"It's just an observation. I didn't mean anything by it." Because I know more than anyone that we sure as shit cannot go there.

"Yeah, okay. I'm sure you also don't mean anything by the fact that you have no idea whether or not you're actually attracted to me," she says and leans back in her seat. She slowly folds her arms in front of her and meets my gaze.

I should have known she would come right out and ask me what my deal is. No hesitation in her voice at all. If she wants to be blunt, so can I.

"I have to keep myself at a distance in order to keep myself from walking into your office, placing you on your desk, and having my way with you, not giving a damn who might see. I haven't stopped thinking about you all week. I crave you more than I've ever craved another woman in my entire life."

"Oh."

I lean forward, never taking my eyes off of her. "A part of me thinks I should just seduce you. Finally find out what you feel like when your naked body is brushed against mine. That way I can get back to my job and regain my focus."

"Oh."

"But the other part of me is convinced that once I have you, I won't be able to let you go. That I'll be even more addicted to you than I am now once I've touched you."

She swallows and leans forward, just like me. "But you have touched me."

"And that's exactly why I know the side that won't be able to let you go is right."

Beth doesn't reply. She only licks her fucking lips one more time.

"Do you think—" I start to say.

"We should go? Yes."

That wasn't what I was going to say, but her idea is much better than mine. I drop some cash on the table. Beth doesn't say goodbye to anyone as we leave the bar.

Her door slams behind us. The noise is bound to startle someone, but not us. It doesn't even faze me. All we can focus on is each other. Or at least, the way her nails scratch my back gives me the impression that she is thinking the same way I am.

My hands travel from her hair to her neck, over her shoulders, and slowly glide down her sides. When they finish making their way over her perfect, plump ass, I grip the backs of her thighs and lift her, spreading her legs to wrap around me. She knows exactly what I want and her feet hook behind me. I hear her shoes hit the ground, but the noise is quickly covered by the moan coming from deep in her throat.

Our lips move faster, harder, more desperately. She tastes like cinnamon and mint. A one-of-a-kind flavor I'll never be able to get enough of. My hands weave back into her thick, silky hair as I press her against the back of the door. At this pace, we'll being having sex on the kitchen floor if we don't find a room quickly.

I grind my hips into her core and she groans.

My lips kiss hers then move to her cheek, to her ear, and then her neck. From there I kiss down to her collarbone, pulling her shirt aside to reach the top of her breast.

"Maverick."

"Beth," I say, loving the way she says my name.

She pushes me back and slowly I let each leg drop until she's standing. I hover over her, her chest rising and falling just as quickly as mine. Her hands go to my pants, where she pauses.

I tilt her chin till she's looking up at me. Her gaze latches onto mine and she smiles.

"This is a bad idea," she says.

I kiss her.

"It's a very bad idea," I say.

She doesn't waste time as she crosses into the apartment. I flick the lights on just in time to see her shirt drop from her hand. She turns to slide her jeans over her hips, revealing the sexiest, most delectable ass I've ever seen.

My eyes dart from her feet up to a small piece of lavender lace fabric as she stands in the middle of the living room. I allow my view to linger there before I clear my throat and find that she is wearing a matching bra with the perfect set of breasts spilling out.

"Couch? Bedroom?" I ask.

Her eyes flicker to a door, and in one step I'm wrapping my hands in her hair as I pull her mouth against mine.

Our lips never part as I walk her backward through the door she indicated. All while she undoes my tie and unbuttons my shirt, gliding it over my shoulders and down my arms. Once I've shrugged it off, she goes for my belt. Before she's finished unhooking it, I lift her lightweight body into the air and sit back onto the bed. Her body feels like heaven as she rests down against me.

Her hips start to grind, matching the feverish rhythm of our kissing.

"Take your pants off," she breathes into my mouth, barely pulling her lips from mine. My hips press up as I regrettably remove my hands from her silky body to push my pants down.

She crawls off me, reaching into her nightstand. She pulls out a condom and, raised on her elbows against the pillows, she watches as I finish undressing. Then, slowly, I make my way across the bed till my body is above hers. The smile on her face is one I hope I see every day from this day forward. It's the one that tells me this is exactly where I'm meant to be.

I slide the condom on and she lies back, her legs opening for me. I shift between them, place myself at her entrance, and capture her lips with my own as I enter her.

I rock back and forth, slowly, the heel of her foot moving against my back with each thrust. I grip the back of that same leg to bring it higher as I slide farther into her. She moans, the sound vibrating against my lips as her back bends under my touch.

Her hands sneak their way to my ass and grab hard as she pulls me into her. The second time she does it, I speed up.

"Yes," she breathes into my ear. So I go faster.

I slide in and out of her, our bodies slapping together with each thrust. Her head is back, digging into the pillow behind her, exposing her neck to me. I press my lips there while one hand braces me on one side of her head and the other reaches between us.

"Maverick," she says, louder this time.

I rub my finger against her most sensitive spot and feel her walls constrict around me.

"God damn, you feel perfect," I say, removing my hand and turning her face to me. I seal our lips together right as that moment of ecstasy courses through my veins.

Beth's hands fly up to hold on to the mattress, her body stilling underneath me.

I slow to my last thrust. Her eyes are closed, but she's smiling. Pulling out, I roll off her and tie off the condom.

"I really, *really* wish I had more than one of those right now," she says.

"One of what?" I ask.

"Condoms," she answers, her sparkling green eyes gazing up at me.

"I've got us covered," I tell her. And I do, two more times before we fall asleep.

CHAPTER NINE

Beth

I open my eyes slowly, as if their movement might wake someone. I had sex with my partner last night and we didn't get a single fucking thing done on our project. What am I supposed to say to Maverick now? Is he going to take me seriously? Is anyone? Is he going to tell everyone?

I don't move. I try not to even breathe as I lie in bed. I don't want to chance waking him up until I know exactly what I'm going to say to him. This can't happen again. It was a mistake ... no I can't say that. People don't respond positively when you tell them they are a mistake. I've watched too many movies where that has ended badly, and since we work together ... fuck. I messed this all up. What is wrong with me? Slower than a snail's pace, I turn over to wake Maverick.

There isn't anyone lying next to me.

Now I know I didn't imagine the night. I had been drinking, yes, but I wasn't drunk. He was here when I fell asleep and now he isn't.

I slip out of bed, pulling on a pair of cotton shorts and large t-shirt before I head for the kitchen. The aroma of fresh brewed coffee meets my nose before anything else. I guess if he's going to be here in the morning, he's got the right idea to get me some caffeine. I peek my head around the corner to find only Abby. My heart flutters a bit down into my stomach. I hadn't realized that I was smiling till now when I feel my smile disappear.

Abby pauses in mid bite with her spoonful of cereal.

"What's wrong?" she asks and puts the spoon in her mouth before pointing at me with it. "You look sad," she comments between bites. "And I'm sure after the opera show I heard last night, you shouldn't be sad right now. If you are, then I really misheard every single noise."

I glare at her and pour myself a cup. I skip the creamer today. I need this baby strong.

"I wasn't aware you were home," I say, taking the seat to her right.

"Well, I came in just as you and Maverick disappeared behind your bedroom door. I figured you would know I was coming home since you asked as you left the bar and I replied, 'I'll be leaving here in like twenty minutes.'"

"Oh."

"You don't remember that?"

"No."

"Ah well, I don't think my arrival or anything else in this world was going to keep you two from coming back here last night."

"What do you mean?"

"Well, for starters, you two practically glued your faces together for thirty minutes before you finally left the bar."

"I what?"

"Okay, now I think your memory is bad, especially since I know I only served you three beers and one shot."

"I'm a lightweight."

"Yeah, by the way I caught Maverick manhandling you into your room, I figured that out."

"Abby."

"Let's skip all the details and get to the part where I don't understand why you look so unhappy right now."

I shrug. If I knew the answer, I'd consider sharing it, but I don't, so her guess is as good as mine.

"Do I need to march into your room and tell your sex buddy that he doesn't know how to use his shit right?" she asks.

"Abby!"

"Well, do I?" Her tilted head and the tight-lipped frown means she's serious. I kind of like that she's ready to stick up for me. I wouldn't let her do it even if he were in there, but the gesture is nice.

I shake my head, finding the back of her cereal box more interesting than her pity.

"No."

"Are you sure?"

"I'm sure." I sigh. "Even if you did it without my permission, he isn't there."

"He left?"

I nod.

"When? I've been up since at least seven this morning."

Again, I shrug. "Not sure," I say, taking a sip of my coffee. Black is good today.

"What a fucking ass. Does he even know how lucky he

was to be with you last night? Does he know he is the first man you let in your pants in over a year?"

"We didn't cover the basics, but it's fine. This is best."

"Your face doesn't say it's best."

"Well, it sucks, yes, but we work together. It was a smart choice on his part to leave. We don't need the whole hassle of things being awkward at work, especially when we have this project and my whole three-month trial depends on it. I can't mess it up, so this good."

"Lies, but whatever."

I focus back on the Lucky Charm maze before finally pouring myself a bowl. I'm not going to dwell on this. If anything, I'm going to be sad that I won't be getting any more mind-blowing sex. If that's what I was missing, I should have considered begging that Saturday evening in Colorado. Maybe I'd have been having sex this whole time.

No. No, I wouldn't have, and I shouldn't and won't be from here on out. When I get to the office later today I'll tell him just that. Piece of cake. It was a one-time thing to get each other out of our systems. And even though it clearly did not work for me, he doesn't need to know that.

Maverick

Her heels click against the floor as she walks into her office and then to her desk. I listen for the noise from the wheels of her chair, but it doesn't come. Instead, the clicking only gets louder.

I sit up straight and adjust my tie. I shouldn't have fucking left the way I did. But I didn't know what to do. I hadn't slept. I only lay there and watched her sleep. I thought about what she would do in the morning, and I'll admit, I panicked. But right now, I have a pretty good feeling she's about to tell me how wrong my decision was. And I deserve it because I'll be the first to admit what a jerk move I made.

"Good morning," she says.

Her tone is cheerful.

This can't be good.

I don't move as I watch her step farther into my office. Yesterday morning we weren't on speaking terms because she thought I was an ass. Last night we were having sex and now today … today it's like everything is back to normal. To before she thought I was an ass. I don't exactly want to ruin it, so I don't say anything.

"We should set up a time to go over a few of the slides this afternoon. We are a bit behind, so we have some time to make up. We also need to figure out the final arrangements for the Fourth of July event. That way we'll already have the schedule together for Bart at our meeting at the end of the week."

She smiles at me, and, honestly, it looks so … natural that I might be more freaked out than if she had come in here demanding answers. She's not mad at me for leaving? She just wants to get to work? The woman who has always called me out for my crap. I have got to be missing something here.

"Mav, are you okay?"

Am I? Shit … *is she*? She used my nickname.

"Yeah, sure, let's see what you have on your slides," I say, playing along with whatever she is up to.

Fooling around with her was a bad choice on my end. If anyone finds out about it, it will cost me my job. I should be glad she isn't bringing it up, but I'm not. I'm irritated as hell that she's acting like it never happened. I'm fucking good in bed. We were fucking good in bed. There should damn well be something to talk about.

She's talking about the event, which is what I should be focused on, but still, I'm not.

"What do you think?" she asks.

"I think we need to talk about last night." I have no idea what she really wanted an answer to.

Her tongue glides over her lips as she stares at the computer screen, and her chest rises slowly before she twists to look at me.

"What about it?"

"Well, to start, you're acting real unusual about it."

"I'm acting like it didn't happen, Maverick. You know, kind of like you did by leaving before I woke up."

"So you are mad about it?"

"Let's just get to work." She switches the screen to the next slide.

"You know as well as I do that we won't get anything done until we both stop thinking about it."

"Well, I'm not thinking about it, so I guess I'll work on this on my own."

"You're not thinking about how we had sex last night and I left before you woke up?" I ask. I'm not too sure mentioning it one more time is making me look any better.

"Clearly not as much as you are, so why don't you tell me why you left, get it off your clearly guilty conscience, and then you can get back to focusing on work."

"I don't feel guilty, I feel conflicted, and I would imagine in your position you feel the same way."

"Something tells me you're more conflicted than I am."

Her eyes latch on to mine, and I get this swirling feeling in my gut that she's going to ask me why I'm here. Austin has hinted about it twice now and she has yet to ask me why. Maybe she really doesn't care why, or maybe she prefers not to know. I prefer her not to know.

"All right. Well then, can we get back to work now?" she asks.

I wish it were that easy for me.

"You're not thinking about the way I touched you?" I ask.

Her body stills.

"The way I kissed you."

She still doesn't move.

"Or the way I—"

"I think we should finish this conversation in my office," she says before I can complete my next thought.

"Why's that?"

"Because my blinds are already closed and because closing yours right now would be a bit too obvious."

"Too obvious for what?" I ask. My heart rate picks up pace at all the reasons why she would want to be in an office with me with the blinds closed.

"Because if you keep talking to me like that, I can't promise I'll control myself," she whispers.

That should have been my line.

"What are you saying?" I ask. I'm prompting it when I should turn her away, but I can't. Sleeping with her to get her off my mind didn't work. It made it worse. And looking at her right now, where I could take her over the edge of my desk, isn't making my next choice very clear.

"We both have the same goal here. Let's not mess it up. At

work we will work, and when we aren't at work … well, whatever happens stays between us," I say.

"But what if I can't control myself when we're at work?" she asks.

"Then you're going to have to be very, *very* quiet."

"Care to test that theory now?" she asks, backing up toward her office.

Yep, sure am.

I move from my seat to follow her when the last person I ever want to see steps through my door.

"Is this another bad time?" Austin asks. I swear I could punch him in the face right now. He's got that scheming grin on his face like he knows something he shouldn't.

"If you're not here with a mock-up flyer for the event next weekend, then yeah, a better time would be to come back when you have one," I say, returning to my desk. Beth gives me a "you can handle him this time" look and then retreats to her office.

"How's your side of the project going?" Austin changes the topic away from himself because, let's face it, he more than likely didn't do his part and it's a good thing Beth planned ahead for that. She's good at this job. Almost too good, and it puts me off a bit. I thought this would be the easiest job I've ever had. But it's not. I feel like I have no control over myself or what I'm doing anymore.

CHAPTER TEN

Beth

I stuff my purse behind the bar as I prepare for my Friday night shift at the BA. This last week with Maverick has been torture in the complete opposite way that working with Austin is torture. How we managed to resist each other—not an easy task, I might add—is beyond me. But somehow, we did it and right now, I'm thankful to be working somewhere with no stress and no sexual frustration.

"Hey girl, is work going any better?" Sky asks. Luke walks in behind her and slaps her ass before clocking in on the computer. Sky giggles but at the same time acts like it's the most natural action in the world even though she's aware people can see them. If Maverick did that to me at the office, I'd probably freak out and be mortified to show my face again for a day or two. Then again, the environment here versus there is not even close to the same.

I give her the short answer. "Work is going good." Sky

laughs at something Luke says and then she shoves him as he wanders back to the storage room.

So, is this what it would look like if Maverick and I could show our feelings at work? Probably not. A bar and an office aren't the same thing. Besides, I don't really know there are any feelings to show other than the fact we want to shred each other's clothes every time we see each other.

"Just good. That's it?" she prompts me.

I'm not sure what I should say. Maverick and I slept together only once and I already have myself in a fucking mind mess at my big-girl job. I really should start acting more grown up.

"The project is going good. I like what I'm doing there. It will be great to see how everything comes together next weekend. You and Luke are still planning to come, right?" I ask.

"Yep, we sure are. I'm excited too to see what you've done." She flashes me a smile. "As hard as you've been working, I know it will be great."

"Ha, no pressure or anything." I chuckle and start making drinks as orders come in off the printer.

"How are things with Maverick?" Sky pinches her lips together as she stocks the cherry tub in front of her, but she doesn't look at me.

"What do you know?" I ask. *Shit, who all saw us here the other night?*

"Enough to know that it's been a month since you started this job and you are still interested in the same guy, and that's a big deal."

"I think you heard wrong. Maverick's still around because I work with him. That's all."

"Yeah, I'm not so sure about that," she says.

I'm not so sure either, but I'm not telling her that.

"So what happens when this job is over and they can select only one person? What will you two do then?" she asks.

I keep my focus on the beer taps in front of me. I hadn't really thought of it. I mean, only one of us will be employed, but as far as me and Maverick, I don't know. Will he leave?

Beer sloshes over the side of the glass in my hand and I shake all current thoughts from my head. Maverick and I work together and had sex once, that's all. Just because I'm attracted to him physically doesn't mean I have to think about what might happen. It doesn't matter what happens.

I know what I need to do and, no matter what happens between Maverick and I in the meantime, I can't let myself forget that.

Maverick

It's been only a week since we slept together yet I feel like I'm going to combust if I don't see Beth outside of work again. And I don't mean just see her. There's something about this girl. I don't want to go as far as to say I need her because we hardly know each other, but whatever it is, it's damn close to need.

I step into the BA where she mentioned she would be working tonight. She never said to actually come see her—she said she couldn't work on the project because she was busy. Working. At a bar. This bar. And I decided I need a drink. I also called Tyler and invited him to meet me here.

My heart is racing like I'm a damn fifteen-year-old all over again. And it's so dumb because I see her every day and we've had sex, so I shouldn't be as nervous as I am now. If I were coming here for the reason I want, to hit on her and take her home after her shift, maybe my palms wouldn't be so sweaty. But since I'm coming here to explain why I'm in the new hire program and that a romance of any kind should wait till after the summer, because we are both professionals, this is the way it is.

Pushing my nerves aside, I head for the bar. A quick scan tells me that Tyler isn't here yet, but there are plenty of barstools open for me to pull up a seat. A blond, Sky I believe, steps up to grab my order. I saw her the night Beth and I were here but never actually met her.

"What are you having tonight?" she asks. She smiles and makes eye contact, but the moment Beth steps out from a door behind the bar, all my focus moves to her. The way her hair shines, braided to the side. The way she's got on a pair of shorts where the hem ends right under her ass cheeks. The way her legs look in their black tights and the way her chest hugs her t-shirt. When she takes a step toward me, my eyes fall to the tears in her tights and I smile. Just the flash of her milky soft skin peeking out sends every idea of what I want to do to her racing through my mind.

I swallow back the images and think of a drink order to give the bartender.

"Maverick, I presume," the bartender says, and I lean back in my seat.

"Have we met?" Maybe we did.

"Just once and it wasn't a formal introduction. I'm Sky." She offers me her hand and I shake it.

"You going to order a drink, man?" A guy steps up to Sky and snakes his arm around her waist as he stares me down.

"Luke, this is Maverick," she says. I don't miss the way she slowly says my name as if he is supposed to know all about me.

"Oh, hey." His attitude takes a one-eighty and he shakes my hand too. Maybe he does know who I am. I start to grin. Does Beth talk about me to her friends? "I'm Luke. I was—"

"Maverick!" Beth pops up next to Sky. She looks panicked. "What are you doing here?"

Well, I came to tell you that we need to remain strictly coworkers, but looking at you now, I know I don't stand a chance in hell of sticking to my own words.

"Just came out for a drink" is what I say instead.

"Oh, of course," she says quickly. She glances to Sky and Luke, who are beaming smiles at her. "I'll take care of him." Sky nods, walking away.

"I bet you will," Luke says and follows behind her.

"So what can I get you?" Beth asks me, her hands fidgeting together as she watches me.

"Is everything okay?" I ask.

"Great." That's a fake smile. "Beer?" she asks and then turns to pull one from the fridge behind her. She seems almost as nervous as I do.

"Hey man, sorry I'm late. I had to make a stop on the way here," Tyler says, pulling up the seat next to me. "I'll take a Bud bottle," he says to Beth's back.

"Find a new bar, Maron," Abby says, now coming into view behind the bar. She slams the small round tray in her hand down on the bar top as she glares at Tyler. I bet their story is a good one, but I also bet it's not one he can tell me about over one drink, so I'll ask him about it another day.

He doesn't reply to Abby the entire time she's staring him down.

"Are you guys still taking the Brian's family boat out tomorrow?" Tyler asks Beth as she places our beers in front of us.

"Yeah, you should come, Maverick," Luke answers for her.

"No," Beth says.

All of us—me, Tyler, Luke, Sky, and Abby—look at her.

"I mean," she starts and looks at me, "you probably have more important things to do on a Saturday."

"Actually, I don't," I reply. If I hadn't been watching her so closely I would have missed the way the right side of her lips tug up slightly before she captures her bottom lip with her teeth. Fuck. Every time she does that, it sends a zing through my groin.

"Okay."

"Awesome," Sky says.

"We'll meet out front here. Say ten thirty?" Luke says.

"Yeah, I'll be here," I say, my attention still locked on Beth.

After a minute, she licks her lips and shakes her head, stepping toward the other end of the bar. I can't see it, but I know she's smiling.

"So you and Beth, huh?" Tyler asks.

"We work together," I say, but even I don't believe it is the short story as I say it.

"I've known Beth for quite some time, and I have to warn you, she's never had a boyfriend before." He takes a drink of his beer while mine almost sprays out of my mouth.

"What?" I emphasize the t.

"Yeah, it's pretty crazy. When her parents divorced, I think it did a pretty good number on her and her outlook on guys."

I've known many people with divorced parents, but Beth would be the first I've ever known who has let that keep her from a relationship.

"Don't get me wrong—she's had a few flings, but no man has ever won her over enough that she kept him around as anything more. Just wanted you to have a heads up," he adds and then signals to Beth for another beer.

She pops the top off more bottles for him and for me. She's still at my end of the bar when Tyler excuses himself to use the restroom.

"If you don't want me to go tomorrow, I won't," I tell her.

She shrugs. "You can do whatever you want, Maverick."

"You keep saying that, but if it were true, I'd have a whole different type of day planned for us tomorrow."

Beth's eyes light up as she holds back a smile.

"So you've said before," she says and then winks at me.

"I only speak the truth."

"I'll see you tomorrow, and please try to keep your hands to yourself," she says.

"I'm not making any promises," I say. When it comes to Beth Moyer, I have low self-control.

CHAPTER ELEVEN

Maverick

I'm beginning to think that my 95 percent success rate is turning into 95 percent of the time I have no idea what I am doing. Like right now, waiting outside the bar to meet Beth and, of course, all her friends. We work together and we've had sex, yet Beth and I haven't exactly hung out. We're doing things completely out of order, but on the plus side, at least she's still willing to spend the day with me doing something that isn't work-related.

"So, your family owns the company where you and Beth are working?" Conner asks. Luke introduced me to him last night before I left the bar. It's his boat we are taking out today.

He's inside the boat, which is still hooked to his truck as Luke and another guy I haven't met yet hand him coolers to put inside.

"Yeah, my father is the president and oversees the Colorado branch," I answer. "Thanks for inviting me. It's a great day to be on the water." Work is the last thing I want to think about today. I spot Sky pulling bags from her car and rush to grab them from her before someone can ask me another question.

"Thanks," she says. "You just earned that sandwich I made for you."

I laugh. I hadn't even thought about packing food. I was so focused on the fact I am hanging out with Beth that I barely managed to grab the one bottle of water I brought.

"Thanks for that."

I follow behind her to the boat and hand Conner the bags. Another couple shows up; they hug each other in greeting and talk about how excited they are for a kid-free day. Everyone is paired off as a couple. Is Beth the only single woman in their group? I know Tyler told me last night she isn't a relationship type of person, but people change, right?

"Oh, there they are!" One of the girls points across the street where Beth and Abby are walking toward us. Beth is carrying a cooler and looks uncomfortable while Abby is on her phone, arms flailing in the air and brows together. I'd hate to be on the other end of that line.

I jog across the street. Beth's hair is down today, shining in the already seventy-degree weather. She's wearing a plain white t-shirt, a navy-blue swimsuit noticeable underneath, and a pair of torn jeans shorts cut so high a guy doesn't need sun on his face to start sweating. A cool breeze would be really nice right about now. Her legs are long and slender down to her flip-flops. Judging by the way she's grinning at me, we could skip the lake and I'd be just as happy, as long as I could be tangled up in bed with her and those legs.

Without a word, I lift the cooler out of her arms.

"Thanks," she says. "For a moment there I thought you were going to just stare at me."

"I can do both."

She bumps my shoulder as we cross the road.

"I'm glad you came today," she says.

"Are you?" I ask and laugh at the same time. Last night at the bar, the idea looked like it freaked her out.

"Yes, I really am."

She's looking down, but I still see the side of her lips pull into smile as I watch her.

"So, where's Tyler? I thought he was coming with you." I ask. Beth slaps her hand over my mouth so quickly I almost drop the cooler from surprise.

"Shhh, if Abby—"

"I already heard him. Tyler isn't coming," she says loudly into her phone and then taps the screen, dropping it into the bag hanging off her arm. "Don't act so surprised," she says to me. "This is Tyler we're talking about."

Beth's hand is still on my mouth. She's got a tight-lipped smile going as she shakes her head. Is she going to laugh?

"I take it he bailed?" I ask in a mumble behind her hand.

"Ugh, Maverick, really? My hand was there for a reason." Beth rolls her eyes at me and walks off. I can't help but smile. She's damn cute when she's irritated with me.

"Tyler doesn't bail. He gets uninvited. By me," Abby answers.

I nod, not sure if I should pursue it or make this moment even more awkward by changing the subject to sports or something.

"Maverick," Beth calls my name. I glance to her direction

and she waves for me to join her in front of the truck. And I do, without another word to Abby.

"All right," Beth starts, "I'm going to do a quick rundown of everyone here."

"Sorry, man, I thought you'd already met everyone," Luke says before Beth can go on.

"Not a problem," I say.

"Okay, you're going to get lost and probably forget someone's name, but here it is. You know Sky and Luke." She points to them, then she points down the line of people, "Conner; his girl, Alexis; Logan, who is Alexis's brother; Sara, who owns the BA and is married to Logan; Kelsey, who is Conner's sister; and Ethan, who is married to Kelsey but is also Sara's cousin. Oh, and of course you know Abby."

She wasn't kidding. I got lost in there on the relationship part, but I think I'll be good to remember all the names. How are we going to fit eleven people on this boat?

"Who is riding with who and who is going to swing by the marina to grab the jet skis?" Conner asks. Twenty minutes later, Beth and I are in the back of Conner's truck and headed to the lake.

"How often do you guys come out here?" I ask. I'm sitting in the back of the boat with Luke and Conner while the girls are at the front. Logan and Ethan are off somewhere on the jet skis.

"Not as often as we would like, that's for sure," Conner says. He and Luke then go into a discussion about a bookstore and something about fire damage. I listen for a bit, but my attention immediately shifts when I catch Beth watching me. She smiles, not even trying to hide the fact that I caught her staring, the same way she did when I first saw her back in the bar in Colorado. If I had known then that this woman was going to make me do things I had no control over, would I have followed her outside that night?

One of the girls must have said something funny because Beth's head falls back and her mouth opens with a big laugh. The sound pierces my heart, and I know right then that I would have done anything to be in this woman's line of sight.

"Who's up for tubing?" Conner asks the ladies.

"No, no, I don't want to get my hair wet today," Sky says, the other girls nodding in agreement.

"I'll go," I say.

"We have wakeboards if you would rather do that." Conner points down to the nook in the hull of the boat.

But the tube is already aired up and ready.

"This will be fine."

"It's big enough for two people, if ah … if you want someone to go with you." Luke's eyes dart to Beth. He leans back in his spot and smiles.

"Funny thing is, about this time last year, this guy would have been telling you to run." Conner laughs and smacks Luke's back.

"Oh, I would not have," Luke argues, popping the top to a soda and handing it to Sky.

"True, you wouldn't have even come today."

Luke's head tilts as he shrugs and then nods. "So, alone or doubles?" he asks me.

"Beth." She looks up at me. "Want to join me?"

"No thanks," she says simply.

"Scared?"

"No."

"Then what is it?"

"I just don't want to get in the water."

"I can bribe you." I grin and wink at her.

She copies my grin, crosses her legs, and leans back against the cushion of her seat. "You don't know me well enough to know what I could want that badly."

"You can take the lead in the radio presentation," I offer. I'm aware at this point that everyone is watching. After my last comment, even the boat slows to a stop.

Beth just stares at me, her lips puckering and her eyes narrowing. I'm as shocked as she is that I said that. Taking the lead is a sign of where you stand against your peers, so letting her do that will give her the upper hand. I'm no idiot; I know she would be thrilled to have the spot.

"I get the left side," she says, standing. The girls do the same so I can lift the seat and hand out our life jackets.

"I have to get a picture of this." Sky digs around in her bag until she had her phone in her hand. Everyone is bustling around now to get the tube ready and in the water as we strap on our jackets and decide who gets to hold the flag and who keeps an eye on the rope. "Beth, where's your phone?"

"I left it at the apartment," she says. In the same way everyone went silent a minute ago, they do it again.

I'm still looking at everyone, confused as shit to what's going on, when the jet skis pull up.

"What's everyone—why do you all look like that? What happened?" Logan asks.

"Beth didn't bring her phone," Sara says.

Logan's brow peaks and that's when I finally ask, "Is that a bad thing?"

"No, it's just, I could show you pictures and pictures of group gatherings and every single one would show Beth on her phone. So, the fact she forgot it …"

Now everyone is looking at me. I'm about to turn to Beth for clarification when her red hair flashes out of the corner of my eye and the next thing I know, she's shoving me over the side of the boat.

The water is chilly when it hits my body, and as I swim up to the surface to catch my breath, I hear the tail end of a very firm "got it" from Beth. Then she jumps in right next to me.

Beth

For fuck's sake, friends. Can't they just act normal around Maverick? I swear, each time I do something out of the ordinary, they must point it out. I know I'm not being normal. Maverick makes me not normal. There is absolutely no need for anyone to bring this to his attention. Ever. At least until I figure out what to do about him and work. I really, *really* don't want to do anything that would cost me my job, and the last thing I want is for people to think I got this job because I was sleeping with the boss's nephew.

I climb on to the tube as Maverick holds it for me with one firm grip, his muscles wet and flexing.

A quick dip in the water wouldn't be the worst idea right now.

"Have I told you yet how glad I am to have you do this with me?" he asks. He's staring at my ass right now. I just know it.

"Well, you did give me an offer I couldn't resist." I adjust my swimsuit top as I settle onto the lime green and white tube.

The tube jerks to the right and my grip tightens as Maverick pulls himself up.

"This thing is going to flip to your side on the first wake. Your weight compared to mine means we are doomed," I say.

"We'll see about that."

I roll my eyes. "Are you ready?"

"More than you know," he says, looking me in the eyes. His gaze flashes to my lips right as I put my thumb in the air. My stomach twists into a knot. I don't think Maverick is talking solely about this water ride.

The boat starts slow.

"Hold tight," I tell him.

"What's the signal to go faster?" he asks.

"Just give them a thumbs up and then a thumbs down to go slower."

"Oh, we're definitely not going slower." His thumb flashes up and he just keeps pumping it in the air.

"Put your hand down!" I try to swat him but have to get my hand back on the grip.

"I will when we get to a good speed."

"Maverick, we aren't going to last long if you keep your hand up."

"Trust me, okay?" His hand goes down and his eyes beg me to comply.

I don't trust anyone except the group we came with easily. I've known them all so long it's hard not to trust them. I'm still getting to know Maverick, but like an idiot, I nod.

The boat takes off and the tube jerks behind it. Conner

whips the boat back and forth, creating waves. We get good air with almost each one, water spraying the two of us, and neither of us can stop laughing. I'm bouncing off the tube like a rag doll while Maverick seems to hold his position well.

I open my mouth to ask if he needs the boat to go faster when we hit a good wave. This time, Maverick's body comes off the tube, but he's still holding on. I know this because that's immediately where my eyes go when my hands begin to slip. Then Maverick's hand disappears from one of the grips. My hand follows right after. I brace myself for the crash when an arm locks behind my back and pulls me back against the tube. I open my eyes to see that Maverick has now latched onto one of my handles as his body holds mine between him and the tube—a grin on his lips the entire time.

"Want me to tell him to slow down?" he shouts.

I just shake my head.

"All right, well—"

Water surrounds me, and my lungs fail to breathe as I swirl under the surface. I'm not under for very long before I'm able to swim to the top. I gasp for a breath, frantically searching to find Maverick. His head bobs up to the left.

"Beth," he shouts, looking the opposite way.

"I'm right here," I say, swimming up behind him.

He splashes a turn and pulls me to him.

There's no time for me to react before his lips crash against mine. His hands hold tight to my sides and it's as though the small current of water forces my legs around his core. I lock my arms around his neck and slide my tongue through his lips. His growls, kissing me harder as his fingers sneak their way under my vest.

"I hate to break this up," Luke says, the boat drifting up next to us. "But those clouds are about to cut our day short."

We look in the direction he points and dark skies are heading our way. We swim to the rear of the boat to use the ladder. I go first but pause to look over my shoulder.

"Do you want to come to my place when we get back?" I ask.

"Yes," he says and then nudges my butt for me to move.

Once we're back in the boat, my eyes never stray from Maverick. Running a towel over his hair or across his body to dry off is such a natural thing to do, but right now it makes my insides scream to take over and tear his clothes off. I almost tell him not to bother pulling his t-shirt over his head, but I don't. He'll figure it out soon enough.

* * *

"I had fun today," Maverick says, leaning against the counter in my kitchen. "I can't remember the last time I just took a day to not focus on work."

It's safe to say that whatever is going on between Maverick and myself, I can't quit now no matter what I think or tell myself. He doesn't show any signs of stopping either.

"Don't you have a hobby or something you do when you aren't working?" I ask.

"I've been so wrapped up in work for the last two years that I sort of put everything I enjoyed doing to the side."

"Where did you work the last two years?"

When he doesn't answer right away, I gaze up from making tea. Why is he looking at me like I just kicked his puppy?

"I've been working at my father's branch."

What?

"You already work at MM?" I ask.

He nods slowly, once, and looks away.

"That doesn't make sense. Why would they put you in this program then?" I ask. Before I was competing against a family member shoe-in—now I'm competing against someone who already works there? I should just give up now.

"Let's not talk about work anymore today, okay?"

The pure worry in his eyes confuses me. What doesn't he want to tell me?

"Well, that's going to be a little hard now."

"Try to forget it."

"Yes, because that will be so easy to do."

"Why do you have to argue with everything? Why can't you just say okay and be done with it?" he snaps.

"Because when someone wants to avoid a subject, nine out of ten times it's because there is more to the story and they don't want to share that information."

He doesn't say anything.

"Exactly," I slam the box of tea bags on the counter. Hopefully, the fact that I'm not facing him anymore will get my next point across. "Maybe you should go."

The room falls silent as he debates whether or not he's going to do as I suggested. He takes a step and I think it's for the door, but it's not. Maverick silences my thoughts with a hug. A simple hug.

"Our lives make no sense right now, but Beth, whatever we have going on together, I can't let it go." His places a gentle kiss on my shoulder and then my neck.

Now. Now would be a really good time to take his "no argument and just say 'Okay'" advice.

His hand slides through my hair, gripping what it can as he spins me around. I don't give either of us the chance to continue this conversation. We kiss like it's our last and strip out of every piece of clothing by the time we've made it to my room.

Maverick breaks the kiss and steps back.

"Turn around," he says.

The command in his voice makes the spot between my legs cheer with desire. I comply and bend over the bed before he can give me his next order.

"Look back at me," he says, his voice deep with want.

With a glance over my shoulder I catch his heated gaze as he smooths both hands over my cheeks. He palms them and grips them with a groan.

"I can't tell you how many times I've thought of you bent over my desk like this," he says.

"I can't tell you how many times I've imagined it," I say.

I see the tick in his jaw as he leans over me, his straining erection pressed against me. He's pushing inside me, slowly. Sex with Maverick feels so good. I don't know why I ever fought something so great. He folds his body over mine, thrusting hard as one squeezes my breast and the other sneaking its way between my legs and rubbing against me. It doesn't take long before I'm crying his name and he's following right behind me.

Later, when we're lying in bed, I can't help but think that working with him and not touching him will be impossible. But somehow, it has to be. No matter how much I crave him, I can't continue to give in. My life depends on it, and whenever

I'm around Maverick or even think of him, my focus is distracted. I can't afford to be disconnected from my work at all. My entire life is in Wind Valley. Maverick's been here for part of a summer. One man can't be worth giving up my apartment, losing my job, or missing my friends.

Can he?

CHAPTER TWELVE

Beth

Hundreds of people surround me as I head across town to the event center parking lot in almost ninety-degree weather. Kids are screaming, cheering, and laughing. Adults are chasing their children and visiting all the local vendors who came out today. TACM is set up on the outdoor main stage, providing music for everyone, and that's where I'm headed.

At first glance, everything seems to be running smoothly, just as Maverick and I had planned it. Austin, too, I guess—I mean, he did make that one phone call … I think. And he did drop flyers off to the more popular places around town like I asked him to. Gyms, banks, local stores downtown, and even at the college. I was just as surprised as Maverick when we met at the coffee shop across from the BA yesterday morning to go over final arrangements—also because we were running later after a long night at my place —and saw the ad for the radio station. I feel proud of the work we have done, and although I'd prefer to not work with him at all, I'm relieved that Austin actually did something.

A good part of me wants to let Austin's father know the lack of commitment his son has had toward this program, but I don't know Bart Mitchell very well and I'm not sure if he would think I'm tattling to get ahead or looking out for the company's best interest, which is what it would be. Also, because if people learned I was sleeping with the other boss's son, I'm not sure they would shout even one good compliment in my direction.

I grab a handheld fan from one of the tables set up through the lot and smile at our ad on the plastic as I wave it in front of my face. I probably should have worn more work-appropriate attire today, seeing as we work for the station hosting the event, but it's too damn hot. I went with dress shorts, a sleeveless blouse—as always—that won't stay tucked in, and open-toe wedge sandals instead. My hair is pulled up into a top bun, and even with it out of my way and my lack of clothing, it's still hot as balls out here.

"Beth," Maverick calls out my name as he jogs up behind me. Dear lord, this day just got even toastier. Not just from looking at him but because of the way he makes me feel. We've been doing whatever it is that we are doing for the past week and I have nothing to complain about. Yes, I'm worried about all the backlash that may come at the end of the program, but I'm trying my best not to let it ruin what I have now. Which is everything I won't have living in Montana if they don't choose me. I'm up against family. A person doesn't compete with family, yet I am, and not to mention, what the fuck about Maverick already working there? I hope to god that man knows this conversation will come up again. And soon. And no using sex to avoid talking about it anymore either.

Maverick scoops an arm around my waist and then kisses the side of my head. I slink out of his embrace.

"Someone could see you," I whisper as I keep walking. He keeps pace with me but isn't fazed by my reaction.

"This place looks pretty damn perfect if I do say so myself," he says.

"Yes, I do believe we pulled it off. Have you had a chance to contact the station? See if any ratings have gone up within the first hour?"

"No, I figured I'd call in the morning. I'd rather wait to see what a whole afternoon and evening does for them rather than an hour. The numbers will be better for our report."

He makes a good point. His reasoning also brings me back to the whole "he already works for the company" thing. I don't know how I missed it before, but now it seems that all of his ideas hint at how much experience he actually has. Of course we shouldn't be checking numbers every hour. We are assisting to make sure the event runs smoothly, after all.

"I was thinking that tonight, when this is all said and done, I might stop by. Of course—"

"Who in the hell is that?" I ask, cutting him off. I want him to come over, but what I sure as hell do not want are the four fucking half-naked woman surrounding the radio station's booth, dancing, on stage. Not in a family appropriate way either.

I take off at a quicker pace, and I can feel Maverick still keeping up with me.

"There has to be some kind of mix up," he says.

"We can't have dancers here. This isn't part of their

marketing plan and these women have nothing to do with the image the station is trying to create. If the owner gets a glimpse of them, he will think we haven't been listening to the values he wants this station to represent. Music for the family."

"We'll get them off the stage. It's going to be fine," he says.

"I really hope your uncle hasn't arrived yet."

Maverick skips two steps at a time as we climb up to the stage. I obviously take each step, which only fuels my anger even more when Maverick reaches the shaggy-haired male who is manning the set up. Does Maverick always have to do things better than me?

The young man's pants hang low and I'm pretty sure he's wearing two different shoes, clearly not giving a shit about his appearance. His shirt represents TACM's logo, so at least there is that.

"I'm just doing what they asked me," he says, holding his hands up. "I normally run the sounds behind the stage, but not today."

"What I want to know is who told you it was okay to have dancers?" I ask.

"Like I told him," he points to Maverick, "the email they forwarded to me said to pick them up. I'm just trying to do my job."

"What email?" Maverick asks at the same time I say, "Show me this email."

The fact that Maverick is calm, not freaking out the way I am, annoys me. If his job were on the line, he'd be freaking out. If this were his first client, he'd be freaking out. But alas, I am reminded that our experiences here are completely opposite. He's probably been in this type of situation before and knows exactly how to handle it.

"Here." The guy hands me his phone. I skim over the parts where his boss replies to the message from MM. Then I see the sender's name and I surprise the shit out of myself when I don't immediately start to scream.

"Why in the hell did you send this message?" I thrust the phone in Maverick's face, demanding an answer.

"I didn't send anything about this," he says.

"Um, your name is right here. I think you did."

"You're joking, right?" He takes the phone form my hand and looks over the screen. "You should know better than anyone at our office that I did not send this email."

"Why should I believe you? We're not even close to being at the same level for this job. You have your secrets and I don't ask you to reveal them. But the fact you don't share them with me is all the more reason to doubt you right now."

"Beth, come on, you know who sent this. He's the one person who wants both of us to fail more than anything."

Austin.

The moment he puts the idea in my head, I know he's right. But I still say the first thing that comes to mind.

"Or it has something to do with why you are here and not working for your dad anymore and you keep using Austin as an excuse."

All right, so that last part was just me spouting bullshit because I'm mad. Austin handles making himself look bad all on his own.

"Well, well, well, what do we have here?"

Speak the devil's name and he shall appear.

"I'm not sure which one of you made the choice for this,

but my father is headed this way right now and I don't expect that he will be too pleased. This is a family event, after all." The satisfied tone in Austin's voice makes me want to vomit.

"Get them off the stage right now," I tell him. He laughs in my face.

"Austin, just do it," Maverick says. He sighs, clearly over this game his cousin is trying to play.

"What's going on here?" Mr. Mitchell asks as he steps up to join us.

"I was just saying the same thing, Father. I'm escorting the women off stage this instant since neither of these two have taken the initiative yet." Austin moves to gather up the girls and then he shows them down the stairs. His father has his back to them now so he isn't able to catch the sight of Austin placing his hand on one woman's ass as his head falls back with a laugh. He's such a pig.

"I'd expected better from the two of you," he says.

"Sir, it was a complete mix-up," Maverick begins.

"I don't want to hear it. All I care about is this running smoothly and our client seeing an improvement in popularity. Let's hope your little mishap doesn't cost us this contract." He eyes Maverick. "You can't afford to have that happen twice within six months."

What? Now I really want to know why Maverick is here.

"Yes, sir," is how Maverick answers. Mr. Mitchell walks away.

"We will catch up later, okay?" he asks, not waiting for my answer before he hurries off after his uncle.

I'm missing a major piece to Maverick's story and if I'm not careful, his ending could ruin everything I have planned.

. . .

Maverick

Fuck. Fuck. Fuck.

How many times will I find myself in this position before I get my shit together? Austin knows my weaknesses and he's going to exploit every one of them in any way he can until I don't have this job. Or any job for that fact.

After the remark my uncle just made, tonight I'll definitely have to tell Beth the full story. It's either that or walk away, and that sure as shit isn't happening. I'd rather her be mad at me, but we have a chance to work it out than to completely step back without ever knowing how things could have been.

I pick up my pace until I'm able to catch up with my uncle.

"Bart," I call out. He pauses and looks back.

"Maverick, I really did expect much more out of you," he says.

"I know, sir. There was a mix-up on how those women came to be here. I think Austin hired them."

He nods. "Yes, I'd agree that makes sense," he sighs. "I really did hope this opportunity would help him straighten up."

He lets out another deep breath. I don't think I need to go into detail on what else his son hasn't been doing.

"We could always spin this to—"

"That won't be necessary, Maverick. I don't believe enough people saw them to make a spectacle about it. I just wish there wasn't something in the first place."

"I agree, sir."

"You know, we all make mistakes, Maverick, and I don't believe for a minute that your father won't take you back. But

I do see why he sent you here. He wants to make you president, and it would be my pleasure to work alongside you but only if your belief in who this company is and what we represent is clear to you. Like myself with Austin, this is your father's way of reminding you of that. You're halfway through it now. Don't mess it up."

"Yes, sir," I say again. Everything he said is right. I don't want to let my father down.

"And stop calling me sir, Mav. I'm still your uncle."

We both laugh at that. It's habit. He's still my superior when it comes to work. I call my own dad sir at work.

"I can do that," I tell him.

"Now, it's a holiday, and as long as nothing else unexpected pops up, I think you and the team earned a break. Enjoy the event." He pats my shoulder and continues on his way.

I peek back to where I left Beth standing. A part of me is hoping she's still there, waiting for me. I know she has a ton of questions. Who could blame her? The question I have for myself now is, what the fuck am I going to do? I can tell myself as much as I want that this will all work out, but the truth is, in the end I will lose either my job or Beth.

CHAPTER THIRTEEN

Beth

I left before the fireworks show and before Maverick could find me. It was the coward's way out, and fully not my style, but something is going on here and I don't like the way it makes me feel. *Unsure.* Unsure about everything in my life. I hate this feeling. It's god-awful and I don't know what to do to make it go away.

I've got my computer and paper in front of me. I noticed a few things that could have gone differently tonight, and not just the stupid dancers who showed up.

I should have known right away Austin had set those women up with the job, but a small piece of me—no matter how much I enjoy being with Maverick right now—might be looking for a reason to end this sooner than waiting for the end of the project. I mean, come on, only one of us gets the job, he's clearly hiding something, and this connection we have, it won't last forever. We all know Austin won't get the job, so that leaves only me and Maverick. And he's already an employee. The whole thing sounds messed up and unprofessional. That's exactly why I avoided him tonight. I want to scream. Scream at everyone for whatever the hell is going on because I seem to be the only person who doesn't know what is going on.

"Your lover boy just pulled up out front," Abby says, walking into the kitchen. Clearly Maverick is keeping his word on coming over. He better not expect to get any from me tonight. Not until I have the answers I want at least.

"Should I let him in, or are you going to let him keep knocking?" Abby asks.

I hadn't even heard him at the door.

"I'll let him in," I say.

I jerk the door open and stand there, arms crossed. I'm right in the center so there is no way he can get past without moving me first.

His shirt is untucked from his jeans and the top button is undone. He gives me a tight-lipped smile that just screams he knows he's got some explaining to do.

"If you let me in, I'll tell you whatever you want to know," he says.

"Am I working hard for a job I'm not even being considered for?" I ask. The answer to this question will determine if I let him in. *Please don't say I've been busting my ass for nothing.*

He sighs. "I don't know what their plan is. I don't even know if I'll still have a job when this is over."

I don't move. I just keep staring at him. Waiting for some sign that he's feeding me some bullshit story or maybe for him to elaborate, but neither happen.

"Fine, I have more questions," I say, stepping back for him to come inside.

"I'd worry if you didn't."

"Why, hello, Maverick," Abby coos from her doorway. "I'll just be in my room if you need me."

Maverick chuckles at her serious tone.

"She'll be fine," he says.

I cross my arms and glare at him. He's speaking for me now … this guy is just full of surprises.

"I wasn't talking to her," Abby grins. "You're the first man she's let back in here after a fight. She usually just cuts it off because no guy is worth the time."

"Abby," I say, hoping she's finished. *Let's just share everything with him.*

"Hey, you used to be predictable. Then this guy shows up and we all have no idea what you're going to do."

I grab a pen on the counter and throw it at her. She closes herself behind her door just in time.

"See, she is already throwing things!" Abby yells through the wall.

"If it helps any, you're the first woman I ever felt I owed an explanation to," Maverick says, watching me from the couch.

His admission stabs at my chest. If this is new for him, too, perhaps I can hold back the bitch in my tone. I nod, because it does help, and then sit next to him.

"Why don't you start from the beginning, and if I have any questions when you're done, we'll go from there," I suggest.

"Okay." He pauses. "A few months ago, my father announced that I was in line to replace him at his retirement.

It's a couple of years away, but still, there were quite a few employees who felt this was inappropriate, considering I've only been there a couple of years and they've been there much longer. They don't think I can do the job. And maybe they were right because about a week before the program started," he pauses again, "I slept with a woman who turned out to be the wife to a gentleman we were preparing to sign a contract with."

Whoa.

Maverick continues to stare at my coffee table as he goes on.

"I had no idea who she was when I ran into her in the lobby. Somehow her guy found out, they showed up at the office, and there was a whole spectacle when I arrived that day. It didn't look good and we lost the contract."

Yikes.

"Later, my father told me that maybe he rushed things by hiring me right out of college. That maybe I need to earn the spot like the rest of them had to. So he sent me here. To prove I am meant for the business."

He finally turns to look at me. He needs this job, but so do I. The pain in his eyes almost makes me not want to ask the questions I still have.

Almost.

"What happens if they do choose you? Will you go back or stay here?" I ask.

"I'll go back and resume my position in Colorado."

"And if they don't pick you?"

"I lose my job with the company."

"Fuck," I say. "That's intense."

"I didn't ask any questions. I didn't even argue with him.

He's right. If I want to be president, I need to prove I'm the right man and that this company can rely on me. He's my dad. I let him down and that's just not something you do to family, you know?"

I'm not sure how I should answer that, given the relationship I have with my family, so I don't say anything.

"So, what happens at the end of the three months? To us?" The question surprises me more than it does him. I don't do relationships. I can keep telling myself that or face the truth: Maverick and I are in a relationship of some kind, and right now, I don't see it ending well for either of us.

"I'm not sure," he says and pulls me close.

I have the good hunch I'm setting myself up for heartbreak.

Maverick

The movie credits are rolling and Beth is soundly sleeping against my side. I'm not sure how much of the movie she watched before she fell asleep, but I hardly watched any, and there is no way I can fall asleep right now. Not with my mind racing over everything. I wish that work and responsibility weren't such a huge factor in my life. And if I've learned anything about Beth in the short time I've known her, it's that she is very dedicated to her work and she really wants this job. When she asked me earlier what would happen when this was over, I didn't know what to say.

"The menu screen has replayed like six times now, and I know you're awake and could shut it off," Beth says, stirring and sitting up. "So what's got you so distracted that I have to listen to the damn song again and watch that silly kid keep dancing on the screen?"

I look up to see the guy from *Super Bad* still dancing, just as she said. I grab the remote and power off the TV.

"I'm just trying to think of a way that this works out for everyone," I say.

"You're still thinking about work?" she asks. "Maverick, you can't dwell on it or bad things happen."

"Bad things don't happen just because you dwell on something." I laugh.

"Yeah, they can. You think about it too long, you start missing facts, and then your story gets mixed up and you think you misunderstood something and that you really can do something about it, but really you can't because it will make it worse."

What is she saying? Is she sleep-talking?

"Oh, don't furrow that brow at me. You know I'm right," she says.

"You could be, but maybe when you've been awake a while you could explain it again in more than one sentence and a little bit more clearly."

She shoves me, grinning as she does so.

"So, what were you thinking about?" she asks.

"How … I don't want to lose my job, but I also don't want you to not get one either."

"Yeah, I think that too."

Something in her tone just now doesn't sound like she's too concerned on the outcome. "But you're not worried?" I ask.

"Of course I am. Getting this job means … it means I get to stay here where my life and my friends are."

"You can't stay here if you don't get it?"

She glares at me; that wasn't the question to ask.

"No, I can't, Maverick, because like you said before, you can't let family down. If I don't get this job, I'll be moving to take care of my mother so my brother can have a shot at his dream job."

She stands and crosses her arms, her hip popping to the side as she looks at me.

"We both have things at stake here, Maverick. Please don't act like you're the only one who will lose something if they don't pick you."

"I didn't mean it like that, Beth. I just, I don't know what to do here. And for someone who made a huge deal about not sharing secrets, don't you think telling me about your family is something you could have shared weeks ago?"

"It's not like you asked about them."

"You've never even mentioned them. I thought that was a sign not to bring it up."

"So I'm just supposed to say, 'Ask me about my family'?"

"I think we are getting off subject here." I pinch the bridge between my eyes.

"I don't want to argue with you."

She sighs and her chin drops to her chest. "Fine." Her response is quick.

"I'd like to think they are going to pick two people," I say, bringing us back to work talk. "But what happens if they don't? What do we do?"

"We find new jobs. We move on. It's going to suck, but it's not the end of the world," she says, clearly looking past what I was really asking.

"Beth, I meant what happens to us? This." I point to her and back to myself. "What are we going to do?"

She shrugs. "I'm sure we will figure it out."

"It's that easy?"

"If we let it be, yes, it is."

"Even if one of us gets it and the other doesn't?" I ask.

She hesitates. "Yeah."

I don't think she even believes her last answer.

Beth takes her seat back on the couch.

"Can we change the subject?" she asks.

"Of course," I say. She's right. This is depressing, and if our time is limited, and it could be, I don't want to waste it.

"Or we could not talk," I say.

Her glowing green eyes look up to mine, and she smiles.

"That's a mighty fine idea."

I capture her lips against mine as she crawls into my lap.

This, this is so much better than thinking about work. Even if it will only make everything feel right for a fraction of the night. In the morning, I'll try to think of a new plan for us. One that gets us both what we want.

CHAPTER FOURTEEN

Beth

The last couple of weeks have been great yet horrible. Everything between Maverick and me is different. Every time I look at him, I can see in his eyes that our situation is tearing him apart. I've also kept my distance at work, knowing now what's at risk for him if someone were to find out about us. Those things are what have made it horrible. The great part? Well, to avoid everything, there has been a lot of sex.

I pour myself another paper cup of Pepsi as I try to cool down in the late July heat. This is probably the hottest summer we have had in years and right now, I'm really wishing there was a pool party gathering instead of the company picnic at Bart's house.

"I'll know for sure if that's even a possibility within the next thirty days."

I hear Maverick's words, but I don't bat an eye or even flinch to look in his direction. Instead, I continue to stand in front of the drink table, adding more ice to my cup, waiting to hear what he has to say. The fact that he admitted everything to me has made him more open about why he's here. But it doesn't change anything.

We both know that whatever happens with the job is going to be a hurdle for us, if whatever we have is still even ongoing. I'd like to imagine that it will be, but if I'm honest, I'll be more than a little hurt if he gets the job. Somewhere deep inside my mind, I'll never know if he got the job because of his family or because I truly wasn't any good.

"How do you mean?" a man asks him. I don't remember his name. He was one of the many people I met when we showed up here today.

"Well, it depends on whether or not my father allows me to resume my position under him," Maverick answers.

"Assuming you succeed over me and Beth." Austin's input silences the entire crowd around them. I can feel all eyes on me. They're burning a hole in the back of my head, just waiting for me to turn around, to have a reaction. I don't really have one. I never expected Maverick to give it all up for me, but then again, I never expected him to assume he would be offered the spot over the three of us. Or maybe I did and I just don't want to admit it.

Because I know they are all waiting, I turn. My eyes find Maverick's right away and his lips tug to the left into a small smile. Even when I'm unsure of my own feelings, he can still make me react. Make me believe it will all work out. All because of a barely there smile. A throat clears, pulling my gaze.

Austin rises from his chair, a beer in his hand and slight wobble to his balance before he regains his footing.

"That's what you think, isn't it?" Austin's words slur just

slightly. A woman whispers something in his ear and attempts to take the bottle from his hand, but he jerks it back.

"I don't need to quit anything. I want to know what it is that this guy thinks makes him better than me."

"Austin, I'm not sure where you got that idea ..." Maverick begins.

"Oh, don't act like you didn't come here thinking you actually had to try. We can all see you're under the impression that you just need to show up and after your suspension period is over, you'll go back to Colorado like none of this ever happened."

A wicked grin takes over Austin's face as he looks at me. "And anything that did happen will be gone." He makes an invisible ball with his hands and slowly moves them apart. "Poof!"

He's really trying to get a reaction from me. Has this entire night. He knows there is something going on between Maverick and me, but what I don't understand is why he wants *us* to make the wrong step. Why doesn't he just out us himself?

If it weren't so silent from the scene Austin has caused, I would have missed the small growl Maverick released with his long sigh.

"Austin, why don't you head inside? I'll be right along behind you. We can discuss whatever you have on your mind in private. Let everyone else get back to the party," he says, rising his glass with a chuckle. "Work talk always has a way of sneaking up at a party, doesn't it?"

A few join him in his laughter while others continue to stare with concern.

With furrowed brows and a grim smile, Austin takes a step

toward Maverick. He tosses his beer into a nearby trash, and I jump when the bottles clank together.

"I better do what you say now, shouldn't I … boss?" he says, right before ramming his shoulder into Maverick.

My hand flies to my mouth. If Austin was looking for a reaction, he's about to get one. Maverick takes a long swig of his beer before slamming it into the same trash, making the same noise. I follow right behind Maverick as he heads to the side of the house after Austin.

"Maverick, don't do this," I call after him. The fact that we haven't discussed work or us further since that night means he probably has a lot of frustration built up. I know I do. But I can't let him take it out on Austin. Not here.

"Go back to the party."

"Not without you."

"Beth."

"Maverick," I say. He isn't the only one who gets to be mad.

He stops and faces me. I glance back at the party that is out of sight now that we are on the side of his uncle's house.

"Don't give him what he wants," I say.

"I can't let him get away with what he just said. It's not right and it's sure as fuck not okay."

I release a sigh and lean back against the house.

"A small part of him might be right, though," I say, fully aware my words could cause a fight. "Please don't hide it from me."

"You're kidding, right?" he asks, hands on his hips, the same frustrated gleam in his eyes.

"Maverick, your plan this whole time has been to come

here, get the job, and go back to Colorado, right?" I ask. I know what my next step is, but does he know his?

His chest heaves with each breath as he stares at me. He licks his lips, opens his mouth, but nothing comes out. One hand rubs the scruff on his chin as the other points at me. Again, his mouth opens but nothing comes out.

"Fuck," he groans, running his hands through his hair and spinning around as he kicks the dirt. "I don't know. I mean, it was … is."

"Even after you and me," I say, the last word coming out in almost a whisper as I hold back the lump in my throat. A tear slips over my cheek as I watch him at war with himself, his hands clenching and unclenching. He looks as though he's in pain, and it sounds as if he can't catch his breath.

We both knew at some point we would be forced to finally have this conversation, holding nothing back. I just never thought it would turn out this way.

"Maverick."

"I had no idea that I would meet you when I came here." His words are calm as he slowly turns to face me. "But one thing is certain: I never once imagined what my life would be like from here on out without you."

He steps toward me. "No matter who gets this position, promise me we will still be us and we will make it work."

More tears fall over my cheeks. If I don't get this job, I'll be gone. Away from here. I think he's forgotten, and it's okay. My life isn't his to worry about. He tilts my chin to look at him.

"Beth, I've fallen so hard for you. Please tell me that we will be okay." His lips are warm as they press against mine. I kiss him back, my lips opening for him to slip his tongue through. Then his body is flush against mine and his hand is in my hair, tugging gently until I tilt my head just enough to deepen the kiss and for his other hand, the one cupping my face, to swipe away a newly shed tear.

"Maverick," I break the kiss, "that's a hard promise to make when I don't even know what we are."

"What?" His eyes search mine. "How could you not know?"

"Well, I mean, we've kept everything between us a secret, so I'm not exactly sure what that means."

"Do you want to tell people?" He kisses me quickly. "Will that help define us?"

"I would love to stop sneaking around, but just because we tell people doesn't mean this is defined."

"You're my girlfriend," he says so simply.

"No, I'm not."

"Yes, you are," he says and that same sexy smile is back. "I know you will have some rebuttal. Some excuse on why you can't have a boyfriend. On why this won't work. But you'll be wrong about it all. I'm crazy about you, Beth. So absolutely crazy out of my mind about you."

I don't have time to reply before he's kissing me again. His hands run over the outside of my thighs until he reaches my ass, lifts my legs around him. Pressing his body harder against mine, he freezes.

"Say you want this too, Beth. Me, you. Everything that comes with it. That we will make it through whatever life puts in our path."

His words pierce my heart, and it's like my body and my lips have a mind of their own.

"Okay," I answer, kissing him hard. "We will make it work."

Everything else—work, my family, his family, the party, the fight with Austin—are gone. It's just us. And although my heart feels like it made the right choice, the wheels in the back of my mind won't stop turning.

If he wins, I'll be gone. And I'm not so sure I can make it work.

CHAPTER FIFTEEN

Maverick

I'm a lucky man to be given a second chance. With my job and with Beth. I'm not exactly sure how I got to be this lucky. I was making some poor choices and someone somewhere should have made me suffer a little longer while I learned from my mistakes. And who knows, maybe risking my job to be with Beth is what's going to bite me in the ass, but it's worth it. She's worth it.

The early morning sun is peeking through the blinds. The small ray falls across Beth's features where I find myself tracing her skin with my free hand until she stirs awake.

"Somehow, you're the only person who can wake me before seven thirty and I don't want to bite your head off," she mumbles, her face in the pillow.

"That's because I have a much better peace offering in the morning than everyone else," I say. "Plus I have another idea for those handcuffs we used last night." My heart about stopped when we got back to my place after the barbeque and she pulled them out of her purse. This wonderful woman is just full of surprises and she's all mine.

"And what's that?" she asks.

With the same hand that was caressing her skin, I tickle my fingers down her back and over her ass. She moans, her body stretching into mine as she inches closer to me. She's still naked from last night, which is working out to my advantage right now.

When my hand is splaying over her right cheek, I move in one swift motion to position myself on top of her. She gasps with excitement, a wide smile peering up at me.

I nudge her legs apart with my knee and settle myself between them. Her back bows and her hands grip the sheets as I kiss my way down the front of her body.

Her taste will never get old. Each time is like the first time. I can't get enough. I want more. I need more.

I take my time, reveling in the way her delicate and soft skin feels under my touch. I heard somewhere that redheads are supposed to have freckles almost everywhere, but Beth is different. Her freckles appear in small groups. Like the three under her left ear, the four that fall into the shape of diamond right between her breasts and the many that scatter just over her right hipbone. She has more, but they are light and hardly noticeable. The everyday person wouldn't notice, but to me, each one is like a piece of art I want to memorize on her body.

"It's not called a peace offering if you're just going to tease me, Maverick," she says with a raspy voice. Her hands trail up my arms to my chest and then around my neck as she slides her fingers into my hair, pulling me down to her. Her lips are soft when she kisses me, but once she slips her tongue into my mouth, my body responds immediately. I grind my hips into her center. Our bare bodies meet and stroke against each other, ready to make a full connection. Beth pulls the cuffs off the nightstand and beams a smile at me.

Until last night, I never thought sex with Beth could get better. Something changed within the last twenty-four hours. Not just her, but with me, too. Perhaps making our relationship official took some stress or worry away. Whatever it was, I don't mind even in the slightest.

Adjusting my body, I thrust into her. She groans at the motion, dropping the cuffs to the floor as her head digs back into the pillow. This right here, having her under me and her body moving magically with mine, is a feeling I never want to let go of.

I'm just about to latch her left wrist to the bed when my phone rings loudly on the nightstand. Without taking my eyes off her, I silence the noise.

It rings again.

I silence it.

It rings once more.

"Just answer it." Beth leans up on her elbows with a sigh. "Then we can resume," she says, kissing my cheek gently.

We break apart while I sit up. My heart sinks the moment I see the ID.

"Dad, is everything okay?" He usually never calls me this early. Something must be wrong.

"It's fine, Maverick. Is this a bad time?" he asks.

"Actually …" I begin, because yes, this is a bad time, but no, I'm not going to say it's because I'm having sex.

"I won't be but a minute, so come let me in," he says.

"You're here?" I stand swiftly, looking around the room for the clothes closest to me. I find a pair of jeans and tug them on and then grab a t-shirt from my top dresser drawer and pull it over my head.

"Yes, I am."

"I'll be right down," I tell him and then press end, tossing the phone on my bed.

Beth is now out of bed as well. She, too, is putting on some clothes, but she isn't nearly as panicked as I am. Which I shouldn't be. *I'm not.*

"You don't need to hurry," I say, stupidly, since she isn't.

"All right, I just figured he is your dad and I should meet him." She buttons up her blouse. "I mean, I thought it would be over dinner when I don't have mid-sex hair and flushed skin." She slaps her cheekbone lightly as she looks at herself in the mirror about my dresser.

"It's fine if you want to wait," I say, kissing her forehead and leaving the room. I don't hear her behind me, so maybe she decided to hang back. But it's also fine if she wants to meet him now. *It is.*

"Dad," I greet him once more as I open the door to my apartment. He squeezes my shoulder as he steps inside.

"Your uncle has said nothing but great things about you since you've been here." He walks into the kitchen and points to the coffeepot. "It's nearly half past eight and you haven't even made coffee yet?"

I shrug. "I was catching up on some sleep. I'll make some now."

I start the pot, watching from the corner of my left eye as Dad takes a seat at the table, his jacket draped over the back of his chair. I also glance right to see if Beth is coming downstairs.

"I can't tell you how proud I am to hear how well you're

doing. From everything I've heard, it's beginning to look darn clear that you understand your mistake. That you accept it and are ready to move past it."

I knew sleeping with a client's wife was a mistake the moment it was too late to take it back. I just hadn't expected it to blow up the way it had. Now though, he's right. I want to move past it.

I am past it. This is a completely different situation.

"At this rate, you'll be offered a spot here in no time and then we can transfer you back to Colorado," he says.

"I've been meaning to talk to you about that," I say, the coffee brewing behind me. The smell alone is waking me up. "Do you think Uncle Bart would be willing to offer the job to more than one? I mean, if I'm going back to Colorado, won't they need someone here?"

The moment the words are out of my mouth, my heart sinks. If they offer me the job, would I actually return to Colorado? Beth wouldn't be there. So, no, I wouldn't. I'll take the assistant job and stay here with her. But then she won't have a job and I won't be in position for president. *Shit.* If life wanted to get a bit less complicated right now, I would be okay with that.

"Are you saying you don't think Bart is going to select you? You've been the project director for over a year now; how could you not succeed in such a beginner's position?"

He fires the questions at me, leaving me no time to answer in between or explain anything to him. Tell him about Beth. After he makes a comment about keeping my work and my personal life separate, my mind blanks. Then Beth is standing at the bottom of the steps and I still haven't answered him.

She clears her throat.

"Hello." She smiles brightly. She's got her jeans back on, rolled up at the bottom, the same heels that I made her keep on last night; her blouse is tucked in neatly, and her hair is pulled into a bun on top her head. She's gorgeous. "I'm Beth."

My father meets her hand with his own. "Bill Mitchell. It's a pleasure." He gives me a side-eye that screams, "This better not be what I think it is." I want my job and I want Beth. I can't pick.

"How, may I ask, do you know Maverick?" he asks.

Beth's smile is beaming as she looks between us. "I'm his …"

"Coworker," I say, cutting her off.

Her smile falls and my heart leaps into my throat.

We all stand there for a moment in silence. Beth is the first to interrupt.

"Well, Maverick, I left those papers for you on your desk. Thanks again for allowing me to stop by so early," she says, not a skip in her voice or anything to hint she's upset. Which I've learned means she will probably never speak to me again.

I can't believe I just said that. I know it was wrong and yet I still don't try to stop her when she walks past me, meeting my gaze so that I can see how much I've hurt her. And I still don't stop her when she closes the door behind her.

"You'll need to watch out for that one, Maverick." I look back quickly to Dad. Was it that easy to figure out? "Beauty and brains is a deadly combination, and if you're not careful, her clear determination to be working on a Saturday morning while you're just rolling out of bed might be what keeps you from this job."

I nod.

He has no idea.

CHAPTER SIXTEEN

Beth

I'm an idiot. A complete idiot. I can't believe I allowed myself to think for even one second that everything was going to be different with him. He fooled me. And for what? Maybe it's all part of a plan that earns him the spot.

Ugh, I can't keep referring everything back to that. I knew the risks of being together, but that was his father. Wouldn't he want his father to know the truth? If anyone is going to be supportive, to see his side of things, family would be it, wouldn't it?

What am I even saying? I'm the last person to talk about replying on family. Either way, what Maverick did was not okay.

Abby's car was gone when I got home, so I slam the door behind me. I'm alone. That's good. My friends have maybe seen me cry three times in the entire time I've known them. I'm not about to let anyone see the tears streaming off my cheeks right now.

My heart aches. I've never known a pain like this. I've made it only from his place to mine, yet I've gone through a point where I couldn't breathe, I wasn't sure if my hands would stop shaking, and I wasn't sure if what just happened was real. Denial—I think that's what it's called.

Now though, I just want to curl up and cry because everything I thought was good wasn't.

I set my purse on the table and lay on the couch. I pull one of the brown suede décor pillows to my chest and begin to sob. Even through the god-awful noise I'm making, I can hear my cell phone vibrating against my keys inside my purse. It's been ringing since about halfway here. I know it's him even though I haven't actually looked at my phone. I don't need to. I'm not going to answer it. What would I even say? What could he possibly have to say to me?

For once, I have nothing to say. Nothing to argue. There is no excuse for him calling me a *coworker* when not even twenty-four hours ago he was telling me I am his girlfriend.

The noise stops but my tears don't. How have my friends gone through multiple boyfriends before they found their husbands? I hope this pain doesn't last long and the moment it's over, I'm going back to vetoing all relationships. My life was so much easier then—a whole two and half months ago.

"Hello, hello," Abby calls out when she bursts through the door. Well, she might not have done that, but it sure as shit sounds like it when the door bounces off the wall. Either that or I'm jumpy. Probably a mix.

I sit up, wiping away the tears and hoping that the makeup I'd managed to salvage from last night isn't smeared all over again. I also take a deep breath to halt my crying.

Fuck, why can't I stop crying? I hardly knew him.

"What's wrong?" Abby asks, rushing to sit next to me. She pulls me into her side and her touch is a new button that sets me off. I start crying all over again.

"Tell me what happened. Did they already choose someone for the job? Oh my gosh, they didn't pick you. Those assholes." She seethes for me. I like that she assumes it was the job. She had that much faith in him, too, it turns out, so we were both wrong.

I give a crap attempt to sit up.

"It wasn't the job," I clarify. Although I wish that were the reason because admitting I'm a hot mess because of a boy is going to be a first for me. "Maverick is an ass and he isn't welcome in our apartment anymore."

"Whoa, straight to eighty-sixed, huh? He must have messed up really bad to get that."

More like he basically told me I was his world and followed that up by begging me to commit and then poof, just like Austin said, everything between us vanished.

Oh my god, Austin is smarter than me. He knew exactly what was going to happen. He tried to warn me and I was so mesmerized by what I thought was right that I let this happen.

"Now, now, take a deep breath or you're going to start hyperventilating, and I'm not so sure there is anything in the world that could be that bad."

"You're just saying that because your heart feels no pain," I say.

"Hey now, that's not true. It hurts looking at you and your big red puffy eyes right now."

Ugh.

"Yeah, but I've never seen you cry over a guy before," I say. "You ditch and switch them before they can hurt you."

And now Abby is smarter than me. What the fuck did Maverick do to my brain?

She laughs. "I don't *ditch and switch* anyone."

"Still, I should have never believed anything that came out of his mouth."

Everything he said sounded so right and like he meant it. Maybe I missed something and I'm overreacting.

No.

I can't be one of those girls. He did wrong. I can't make excuses for him because I don't want to accept this.

"I'm sure he meant most of it. Tell me what happened, and maybe an outside opinion will help get a better perspective," she says.

Yeah, that's a good idea. I'm obviously clueless when it comes to men.

"I better start with yesterday at the company picnic when—"

"Beth!" His shout is followed by a single knock.

"Ballsy. I'll give him that." Abby looks at the door.

I jump up and rush to it like he's going to open it and come in before I get to tell him to go away.

"Beth, please just let me explain."

"Pretty sure you lost that privilege when you acted like I was nothing to you," I argue back.

"Ouch, yeah, that's going to be a tough one to come back from," Abby adds and then wanders into her room, closing her door.

"I know, I know. I just … I wasn't thinking. Please let me come in."

"No."

"Fine, but we still need to go over this presentation and

who will deliver each section to TACM."

"Don't weasel your way in here with work talk," I snap.

"I'm not being a ... weasel. If you don't believe me, open the door a crack and I'll hand you the printed slides. You'll confirm I'm not lying and then we can put them in order. It'll take five seconds. I'll go home, label the slides in the presentation, and sort them for tomorrow," he says.

I stare at the door handle as if it's going to give me the answer. It would be really nice to focus on something else for a few minutes, even if it is with Maverick. I still need to put work first.

If I'd have been doing that in the first place, I wouldn't be standing here with a broken heart.

Maverick

"As much as I would love to dive into work right now, this isn't anything we can't discuss on Monday morning, Maverick."

My heartbeat picks up.

Yes, I'm being a weasel as she called it, but how else am I going to get in there to talk to her? I have to make this right.

"Beth, please," I plead with her.

"I don't do this, Maverick!" she shouts through the door. "I don't have fights and make up. I fight and move on. It's for the best."

"I disagree."

"Well, you lost your vote when you called me your *coworker*. Perhaps I'll start calling you ... jackass or ... no, lying sack of shit."

"I messed up, okay. I know I did and I'm so, *so* sorry,

Beth." I rush the words out before she can argue with me to leave, again. "Please, open the door. Please."

Please.

She comes into view slowly; I let my gaze take her in from bottom to top, and my heart skips. Her eyes are a bit puffy and red.

As though my heart can't think of enough to do right now, it drops to my stomach and then jumps back up my throat. I did that. I made her hurt.

I reach for her, but she steps back.

"Please, Maverick," she hesitates, "don't."

I deserve that.

She doesn't step aside to let me in, but I'll take it. She opened the door. That's all I need.

"I'm sorry," I repeat, because I don't know what else to say.

"I know you are," she says, lifting her head to look at me. She licks her lips and I stand frozen as I watch a tear fall. "But I don't think there is anything you can say to me that will make this better. You made your choice and so have I. Now, I need to make better ones."

"Just let me explain—"

"I feel like that's all our relationship has been, Maverick. Me listening to you explain everything. I'm tired of waiting for you to be open with me. I just want honesty, and it's clear that somewhere inside you're scared to admit the truth to people."

"I am honest. I'm just so fucking tired of disappointing people. Until you, my job was everything to me. President has always been my goal, and even though I still want it, other parts of my life have changed and I obviously don't know how to handle it. I know how to sell product to a client, to bargain my way to the best deals, to control a room full of fifty employees, but this … you and me … it's new to me."

She sighs, leaning against the frame of her door, still not allowing me inside. "It's new for me too."

"I should have just told him. I know that now." God, I want to reach for her. Pull her into my arms and never let go.

"Did you tell your dad the truth after I left?" she asks.

I want to look away because she isn't going to like my answer, but I can't. I shake my head.

She releases a long sigh and drops her chin to her chest.

I know how it looks. No one has been harder on me than I have been to myself over this whole fucking stupid situation. But when my dad said keep sex and work separate I gave him my word. Letting him down is what got me here and yet I'm here and letting him down all over again.

My mother would be so unhappy with me.

Be a hardworking, trusting, and considerate man, Maverick. And most of all, please keep your father happy. It shouldn't be hard to do; you've always made him proud.

"How do you expect me to believe you when you're here right now saying you know you did the wrong thing yet you haven't done anything to make it right?"

"I have a lot at stake here and I—"

"I don't want to hear what you have at stake anymore!" The rise in her voice catches me off guard. "I'm sick of listening to what this job has done to you, Maverick. I have things to lose too. They may not seem as huge to you, but they are big to me. And if you can't figure that out, then you never truly cared about me, and for that, I think you should leave."

She steps back, ready to close the door.

"No, I do know. I just … fuck, I can't even say the right thing right now. I'm trying, Beth. I'm trying so hard to make this work for everyone. I also knew the consequences of being with you. I know it could cost me my job and yet here I am. I want to make this work."

She sighs loudly, shaking her head and folding her arms in front of her as she leans on the wall. At least that looks like she might be settling in to talk more. I mean, I hope that's what it means.

"Maverick, if that were true, you'd have told everyone else the truth, too."

"I'll tell them all tomorrow. Every last one."

She releases a long sigh. "I really want to believe you."

"So do—trust me. I know I messed up, I know what I did was wrong. Let me fix it and I swear to you, I'll never let you down again."

She shifts on her feet, focusing on something behind me. I don't look to see what it is because if I do, I might miss the signal that she's going to give me one more chance.

"Please," I beg, reaching for her hand and lacing our fingers. She jerks her hand back.

"Actions speak louder than words, Maverick. It's an old saying, but right now, those words haven't never been so true. You want this to work, prove it. Until then, I want to focus on nothing but my job."

Her door is closed before I can say anything more.

My heart pinches with each step I take away from her apartment. It's when I get to my car that everything finally clicks.

For the first time in a long time, I know exactly what I need to do.

CHAPTER SEVENTEEN

Maverick

"Good morning," I say cheerfully to the man who shares the elevator ride up with me. He just nods and gets off on the second floor where an investment firm is located. If he were about to do what I'm about to do—tell my dad the truth about me and Beth and then win my girl back—he'd be in a pretty good mood too. Today is the day I put everything out there. No more sneaking around with work or Beth. The last two and a half months would have been a lot easier if I'd have done this from the beginning. It just took me a bit longer than most to put my priorities in order—starting with Beth. She wants honesty, well, I'm about to downpour it.

"Good morning," I say, greeting Ann as I pass her desk. "You should call my father. He misses you." She gasps as I pass another desk, knocking on the top with my knuckles, and smile at the guy behind the computer.

"Good morning," I say to him as well as I continue to

make my way toward my office. I have no idea what his name is.

What I do know is that my father will be here in just under an hour and after that, life will be good. But first, I need to get rid of the leech standing at my office door.

"Well, what could possibly put my cousin in such a good mood?" Austin asks as I approach my door. He's leaning against the frame with his arms crossed and a smug smile on his face. He isn't really interested in what he just asked me. He's here for something and I have a pretty strong feeling I know what it is.

"Well, it isn't you," I say and his head jerks back. Damn, I should have tried this blunt thing a long time ago. "I have a long list of things to take care of today, Austin. So, please, get to the reason why you are here," I say. His eyes narrow, but he gets right to it.

"I'm pitching a separate proposal to TACM, and if my schedule is correct, I'm doing it an entire hour before you and Beth will be presenting yours."

Tomorrow is the day we present. Then the radio station has forty-eight hours to decide if they want to hire us. After that, MM chooses who—Austin, Beth, or me—they will hire. Two proposals to choose from was never an option.

"That wasn't part of the program. Yeah, you could work separately, but we pull our assignments together and pitch as one. You know that," I remind him.

"My father was happily open to the idea of switching things up this year. He's always been a competitive man, as you know, and he's looking forward to hearing what we all have to offer."

I take my seat behind my desk to absorb the pile of bullshit he just laid out. "By all means, please proceed with pitching to TACM before Beth and myself. With the research and hours Beth and I have devoted to them, I have no doubt TACM will accept our proposal."

He huffs.

"Now if you don't mind—"

Where did this envelope come from?

The issue with Austin is pushed to the back of my mind as I stare at the unfamiliar item on my desk. Not because its manila color makes the bold, black letters of my name stand out, but because it's leaning up against a picture I have on my desk. A picture of me and Beth. A picture that was in my drawer and before now didn't have a frame. I don't think even Beth knows it was in here. But this envelope is good sign someone has seen it.

I grab the folder. Inside are more photos of me and Beth. Shots no one should have. Or have ever taken. I shake them back down to the bottom without even pulling them out but keep my grip on the letter that was included with the pictures.

"Everything okay?" Austin asks.

"Fine," I say with a grunt and shove the folder in my top drawer, locking it once it's closed.

"Are you sure? You're looking a little pale. Is it because I mentioned the project?" he asks.

Forget the presentation. Being as blunt as I'd like to be right now could get me fired.

"No," I growl out.

Austin stands straight and sticks his hands in his pockets.

"All right well ..."

I don't hear anything else he says. My focus in now on the

crimson-haired beauty that just walked by my office. The one who has no idea how upside down this day just turned.

"So, yeah?" Austin asks. I remove my eyes from Beth and find him glancing in the same direction.

"Yeah what?"

He turns to me once again, slowly. "Things with Beth are working out all right even after the picnic where you told everyone you'd get the job and she wouldn't?"

Breathe. Breathe. Breathe.

"I don't think that is anything you need to worry about," I tell him and enter my password, lighting up my computer screen.

"You're not just saying that because you seem to have taken a liking to her more than other employees around here? The way you know your dad wouldn't approve of—kind of like the last woman you fooled around with?"

I keep my eyes trained to the computer. My cousin has got to be the dumbest man I know.

"Nope, she's good at her job. Simple as that," I say, refusing to give him the reaction he is working toward.

"Well, I guess I should let the two of you get back to work. Big day coming up. Don't want to mess it up."

Once he's completely left my office, I move to close my door and then I close the door that connects with Beth's office. That door has only been closed once in the time she has been working here.

Knowing I'm closed off from everyone else, I pull the folder out of its drawer. Beth's naked body and long legs are in every photo. I'm not much more clothed myself. I'd prefer to punch the person who took these photos, but my fist slams down on the desk, hard. Some sick bastard has been stalking us to get these photos, but what concerns me the most is who they've shown them to or who they plan on showing them to.

Dropping the photos with a flick of my wrist, I lean my chair back and rub my palms into my eyes. I don't even want to guess what is in this letter. It can't be anything good. I couldn't care less about what it says about me or if they are threatening my job; it's Beth I'm worried about. She's worked so hard, only to get caught up with me and have all of it ripped out from underneath her.

I sit forward and unfold the white piece of paper.

Sleeping your way to the top is not how business it done, and she's about to learn firsthand. Unless, of course, you finally do the right thing. End it. Now. I'll know when you've agreed and only then can I promise that these photos won't be revealed to anyone else. Which is more important: your future or hers?

Fuck.

CHAPTER EIGHTEEN

Beth

"Good morning, everyone," I greet the management team of TACM with a smile. I'm a bit shocked at how comfortable I feel leading this presentation. More so since Maverick has yet to show up. I'm blunt, yeah, and I work at a bar, so speaking in front of a bunch of people shouldn't faze me, but I honestly thought that I would be more nervous about this. This is, after all, the presentation that will ultimately decide how my career plays out from this moment forward.

I have no idea how Austin's presentation went this morning. I just hope mine and Maverick's will be better. Him showing up … well, that would be a start. Did he not hear a word I said the other night? *Actions speak louder than words.* And right now, I'm feeling like I just got a big fuck you from him.

I receive a nod from each of the eight people sitting in front of me, six of who are from the radio station. The other two are Bart Mitchell and his assistant, Gail. Mr. Mitchell nods his head once more, pointing to the white canvas behind me that will display the presentation.

"Ms. Moyer here and Maverick, who is running late, have been working day and night on a package for you. If the rumors around the office are true, you will all be quite impressed," he says.

Hopefully, I hid my wide-eyed panicked response at the word *rumors*. I instantly assumed he was going to talk about me and Maverick and the relationship we shouldn't be having as coworkers. I give myself a moment to let my racing heart regain its normal pace, all while maintaining a reassuring smile that I can do this.

"When TACM originally contacted Mitchell Marketing, you spoke of wanting to regain your followers. Build your following back by reminding people what kind of station you are," I pause, for effect, of course. "While that idea is the perfect goal, reminding people of who your station once was is not."

A few faces trade annoyed glances, but I don't let it distract me.

"Times are changing, along with the people in this town. No one wants to be stuck in the past, they want the new and hip and fresh voices. They want to hear a station that's going to pump them up. A station that brings excitement to their day before eight in the morning. A radio station that stands for something."

This time, there are a few squinted eyes as they keep listening.

"Over that last couple of months, I've done research to find out what the people want. You know what your station wants, now it's time to see how we can combine the two."

I lean forward, waking the screen of my laptop, and then double-click on the drive with the presentation. The file opens and nothing is there. The folder is empty. Blank. Not a single file where there should be many.

I glance up and force a smile.

Holy fucking shit, where is our presentation?

"Just one second," I say as I remove the drive. I flip it over to see the station's initials I scribbled on it with Sharpie. It's the right USB. Maybe my laptop just didn't read it.

I plug it back in and repeat the steps.

Still nothing.

I let out a slow breath and hope it didn't release as loudly as the screams going off inside my head right now. This file has everything I need. My head starts to spin. I don't have a backup. Now my leg is bouncing. Why hasn't Maverick showed up? Did he save a backup? Surely he did, right?

"Ms. Moyer." My head snaps up only to catch the scowl on Mr. Mitchell's face. "Is there a problem?"

"Well, I—"

"Beth," Maverick says, rushing into the room. His quick steps slow when he takes in all the eyes watching him from around the table. "Can I talk to you for a minute?"

"Maverick, Beth is in the middle of a pitch. A pitch you are late for. Whatever you two need to discuss can wait. Now, since you were not able to show up on time, please let her finish."

Maverick's eyes flash wide between me and his uncle.

"Of course. I just have something for her." With his head down as he approaches me, he looks up to make eye contact. Then I see his lips move. He mouths to me, "It's gone."

I twist, pretending to have a scratch, and mouth back one word: "What?"

He pauses when his eyes recognize my glare. Then, before I can think, he is standing next to me, hunched over the computer like I was moments ago. I mimic his stance.

"What do you mean, it's gone?" I whisper.

"It's been deleted."

"By who?"

"Let's talk about this later. Now we need to—"

"Who?" I ask in a harsher whisper. "Did you do this on purpose? To ruin my chances?"

"Beth, no." He sighs and shakes his head. "We need to figure out what we are going to say without the slides."

"That's easy. I have it memorized."

"Then—"

"I do apologize for this." Mr. Mitchell scoots his chair back. "Please forgive me for asking for a moment with my employees."

"Not a problem," a man says. "This was starting to sound a bit too much like the last presentation we just sat through."

This time, I know everyone can see my eyes widen. If it were possible, my eyeballs would fall right out of these sockets.

Austin gave *our* presentation. That's why I was receiving those faces. Does Maverick know? Obviously, he does—he just told me it's gone.

I lock eyes with too many concerned faces, but it's Bart's alone that could make my heart stop. I exchange a glance with Maverick before following him and his uncle out the door. Gail, head down and papers clenched to her chest, is right behind us.

The door barely latches closed before Mr. Mitchell's hands are thrown in the air.

"This is a conversation for my office, but since the two of you have clearly put me in a position where I'm unable to do just that, right here must do."

His phone pings—clearly our situation isn't that dire because he checks it. His eyes widen and then he squints. He motions to Gail and sighs. "Please call security up here. This is the least favorite part of my job."

"Security? This is all just a mix-up. The file somehow was erased. We'll get it back, just give us some time," Maverick pleads with his uncle. He moves to rest a hand on my lower back but I move away from his touch. I don't know what going on with him, but I have good feeling whatever he's done is the reason that file is gone and the reason I'm standing in the hall right now, not landing the contract that should earn me a job.

"Austin stole our presentation." Maverick's tone is clipped.

"I—"

"I believed he was responsible for the women at the event center, but this, this is not something he would do," Bart defends his son.

"I think he would." I join the conversation, my heart jumping up my throat when Bart slowly turns to face me.

Fuck, and I thought I gave some nasty scowls to people.

Mouth is shut.

Got it.

"You've had more than two months. And from what I've seen and heard, the two of you spent more time fooling around with each other than working on this project," Bart continues.

"They what?" Maverick's father's voice from behind us startles us both.

That heart that just jumped my throat has now flopped to my stomach.

"Dad, you know that isn't true. You've seen how hard we have both worked. Beth, especially."

"Maverick, I don't need you to defend me."

"But I am because you didn't do anything wrong." His voice is louder and it only makes his father angrier.

"You're right, son. She didn't, but you did. All you had to do was commit to the job. Keep things … separate." His last word is spoken slowly and with a long sigh.

"Dad—" Maverick's voice is full of warning. "I did. We did. We were able to work together and spend time together outside the office. That's a whole lot of commitment, if you ask me."

I'm too shocked for words at this point. The conversation went from not being ready to present to commitment issues faster than I would ever imagine.

Two of the security men who regularly remain in the building lobby downstairs join us.

"Ms. Moyer here needs to be escorted off the premises," Bart says, and I gasp.

"Me? Why?" A man grabs my arm and I jerk it back.

"Sending inappropriate photos of yourself and another coworker is not how we do business here."

"What!" Maverick and I both shout at the same time.

"I never …"

"Please don't make a scene," Maverick's father asks. Out of everyone here, he shows the most grief on his face.

"But I never sent any photos. I didn't do what you're accusing me of."

"It was sent from your email account," Bart says, motioning again for security to resume their job. "I'm sorry, Miss Moyer, we can't employ you with MM."

Bile forms in my mouth and I'm going to be sick, but I manage a nod. I need to be professional, and screaming my innocence right here isn't going to make this situation better. "At least let me do it without security," I say.

Mr. Mitchell begins to shake his head, but Maverick's father, who is clearly older than Bart, holds up a hand. "That will be just fine," he says.

"Beth," Maverick starts to follow me, but his father stops him.

I'm done with this company, and I am done with Maverick.

Maverick

"Just give me a moment," I say to my father. He sighs for what feels like the hundredth time in the least five minutes but nods.

"Beth, wait," I call out. "Let me explain."

Her steps don't even hesitate as she continues to walk away from me.

"Please, I know this looks bad, but it—"

"Bad?" The word comes out in a growl as she flips around. I almost run into her. "Maverick, this is so much more than bad. This was my first *real* job. A job that meant everything to me. Now no employer is going to see me as a serious worker. Because of you, everyone is now going to think I sleep my way to the top."

"No one is going to think that."

"Really? You're going to say that me? You heard Bart just now. Someone sent pictures of me to everyone here. Where did they get the photos, Maverick? Huh? Can you answer me that? Is that what you need to explain?"

I wish I had an answer other than blaming Austin, but even I don't know how he got them.

The last time I was caught with a woman at the office, I cared only about taking the heat off of me, protecting my reputation in the office. This time it's different. I don't give a shit what Bart or Austin or anyone else makes of our fight. I made wrong choices and I deserve this, but it's different because I don't want this to be the end. I don't want her to leave me. I want what we have. I meant everything I've ever said to her. But right now, she isn't going to believe me.

"Beth, I didn't do this," I say, reaching for her hand. The tips of our fingers brush before she jerks back. My head drops to me chest. I should give her some space, but I can't. What if she needs more than space? I won't be able to handle that.

"Do what exactly, Maverick? You didn't delete our presentation? You don't go making office relationships a habit? You didn't take nude photos of me to sabotage my chances? Or you didn't make me fall in love with you just so you could get everything you wanted, regardless of how it ended for others?" I catch the slight shake in her bottom lip as she glances away. "Tell me, which part didn't you do on purpose?"

I pause before I say another word in the silent tension that fills the air. I didn't mean for any of this to happen. I don't know what happened to the file. I just know I went to view it on the shared drive before our presentation and it was gone. And the pictures … I was late to our meeting because I wanted to confront Austin about it, but he must have left the building after he spoke with the station, because I never saw him.

But after all that, all I can focus on is the part where she said she fell in love with me. I swallow, falling numb at the throbbing ache in my chest. I fell in love with her, too.

"Beth—"

Her hand comes up as she shakes her head. When I hear her faint sniffle, I step for her. Her small frame fits perfectly in my arms and I hold her tighter as I feel her shake. For a moment, I think we can get through this. For a moment, I think we're just having another fight and everything is going to be fine, because there is no possible way things between us can grow worse, but then she shoves me away.

"You don't get to do that. You don't get to do anything anymore. I don't want you to follow me another step. I don't want you to call, or text, or show up at my apartment. I don't want to see you, Maverick."

This time when she leaves, I let her. And I listen to her. For now.

CHAPTER NINETEEN

Maverick

I step into my office and not a second later my father follows me in.

"Maverick, do you want to talk about it?" he asks.

"No," I snap and drop into my chair, twirling around to look out the window. I was supposed to be making things better. Show her how much I wanted this—us. And now, I'm not sure what I can do to get her back. To get her to trust me again. *I'm a smart man, how could I let myself fuck up so badly?*

"Son." Dad takes a seat in one of the chairs around my desk. "Is this job really what you want?"

It used to be. Now, thinking of a life without Beth seems … wrong.

"When I didn't know that there was more to life than having the perfect career, yeah, it was." I turn slowly to face him and he's smiling.

"What?" I ask.

"I felt that way once myself. Almost started my own company. Your grandfather hated that I wanted to spend more time with your mother than at work." He chuckles. "I was ready to leave—do my own thing. All so I could have your mother in my life."

"Grandfather didn't like Mom?"

"Oh he did, he loved her like she was his own daughter. And that was why he came to his senses. He knew she was good for me. She made me strong."

"What does this have to do with me?"

"Simple. The fire I saw in you just a bit ago, that spark you had trying to protect her, it's rare."

"She didn't send those pictures. Someone put them on my desk yesterday morning and threatened both my job and hers if I didn't end things with her."

"I believe she didn't send those pictures either; someone hacked into her email."

"How? No one else believes her." I lean back and rub my hands over my face. *She doesn't deserve this.*

"I believe her because you believe her. You're my son. I trust you."

I snap my head up. "You do?"

"Of course."

"But I thought you sent me here because you couldn't."

"I sent you here hoping you'd learn more. I didn't say in what area. I moved you into the director position so quickly, I was beginning to think I stole a part of your youth. The part where you really focus on what you want to do. And also because you messed up." His brow raises, but he's grinning.

"All I've done in the last few months is mess up. I've made mistake after mistake."

"We all make mistakes, Maverick; the important thing is that you learn from them."

I groan. "Well, I'm sure learning the hard way."

"Sometimes that's how it works, son."

Bart's voice echoes outside my office, drawing our attention. Sounds like the contract didn't go well. Sucks for him.

"What happens now?" I ask.

"Now we contact security, review some tapes, and find out who is behind all this."

That's a grand idea.

"We lost the contract." Bart storms into my office. "Said they needed a more organized firm. One with less distractions. Someone who won't struggle to provide what they are asking for."

"If Austin hadn't stolen our presentation, they could have had that," I tell him straight out. Beth style.

"Bill, I'm sorry, but Maverick can't continue to blame his mistakes on others at this company. I can't offer him this job."

My dad's hand is up, ready to defend me, but I'm quicker.

"So that means Austin gets the job?"

"He's clearly the focused one here," Bart says.

"I'm sorry to hear that." I stand. "Because hiring him means one thing."

"What's that?"

"You're fucked."

Then I walk right past him and out of the office. I hear the argument between him and my father as I make my way to the elevator. I'll have to apologize later for pawning him off on my dad like that.

"It was good to see you, Maverick." Ann steps around her desk to hug me. "I'm going to miss all the excitement around here."

"I'm sure you'll have plenty more here soon," I say. He fucking hired Austin. What an idiot. "I'll see you around."

I press the down arrow and just as the doors open, I hear my name.My dad steps into the elevator with me.

"Dad, I know I should have been focused on work and that I shouldn't have spoken to Bart that way and that I should be in there fighting for this job, but Beth …" I smile, but my next thought crushes my heart. "I can't lose her."

He nods, pressing the lobby button.

"So," he asks, "what's your plan?"

"My plan?" I ask.

"To get her back," he says.

My face must say it all.

"You don't have a plan? How will you win her back without a plan?"

I shake my head.

"I'm twenty-six years old and my father is still teaching me how to be a man."

"Makes me feel young," he says.

We both laugh. And then, I start thinking of a plan.

Beth

The last thing I should be doing right now is driving. Yet here I am, cruising down the streets, barely able to see through my tear-blurred view.

"Naked pictures!" I scream into my silent car.

As if having the first man I love be ashamed to admit there was something between us wasn't bad enough, let's just email some nudes out to the staff.

Fuck.

As much as it hurts to know everything I worked toward was just pulled out from underneath me, it hurts more to know that the first time I let someone in, he betrayed me. Twice.

I trusted him.

I've never told anyone that I loved them aside from my family and friends, and those cases were rare. Maybe I should have, though. Had I actually let a guy in during high school or college, I could have started with a calmer approach to dating life. I could have had someone break up with me or lie to me or even cheat because they didn't want me anymore. No, I have to go and max out the heartbreak box and let the man I love use me for his own personal gain. I let him fool me into thinking everything we had was real. *Three months, Beth. Really.* Three months was all it took to ruin everything I'd created for myself in the last twenty-five years.

I didn't have a destination in mind when I got in my car, but when I pull up in front of Kelsey's home, I know I came to the right place. My closest friends are exactly who I need right now.

I attempt to brush off my tears with my palms, but even without a mirror I know that all I've done is make the smudges worse. Any chance of hiding my emotions right now are a lost cause by the time I reach her door. I don't have time to knock before Kelsey appears on the other side of the door in a hoodie, sweats, and with a messy bun on top of her head as she cradles her newest baby boy, Andrew, in her arms.

"What's going on?" she asks.

"Auntie Beth!" Clara rushes toward me. Her legs are moving faster than she can control and the image of Phoebe from *Friends* running through the park comes to mind. Leave it to a cute little chocolate-headed girl to make me smile when my heart is shattered.

"Whoa, Auntie Beth, you need to fix your 'scara."

That makes me laugh.

"You don't like it?" I ask.

Andrew starts to fuss.

"I'm just going to pass him off to Ethan and I'll be right back," Kelsey says as she leaves the room.

Clara is still shaking her head. "I do like it, but Mommy told me that if I don't know how to use it, I can't."

I remember the day Kelsey told her that. We were outside for a barbeque; Clara and her cousin Jake were inside. We'd all thought they were playing with some of her toys when Alexis went inside for a soda. She came back out to say the house was awfully quiet. Kelsey immediately went straight to her room. Turns out it wasn't the first time Clara got into her makeup, and we learned that day, as both kids stared up at the adults with black streaks all over their small faces, that Clara was no better at putting it on Jake than she was on herself.

"I'd say your mother is probably right."

I plop myself on the brown leather couch and watch as Clara leans over the armrest and blushes before looking away.

"What?" I ask. That face says she's up to something.

"Mommy didn't show me how to use it, but you should ask her."

I laugh hard at her comment.

"I'll be sure to do that," I finally reply.

This time her face is serious.

"What's wrong?" I ask again.

"Can you ask for me, too?"

Kelsey reappears before I have a chance to answer.

"Mommy, Auntie Beth has something to ask you."

"Oh, she does, does she?" My friend's tone is a dead give-away of how well she knows her daughter. The wink she gives as she sits next to me confirms it.

"Aunt Beth, what is it you want to ask me?"

"Well," I begin. A small hand rests on my knee and big, brown eyes watch me with urgency. "It's been brought to my attention that my makeup isn't done properly. I was wondering if you could show me and Clara how to do it correctly?" I ask.

Kelsey's mouth forms a firm line.

"I'm sorry. I can't do that. Only adults wear makeup."

"But Beth is an adult, Mom; I was just gonna watch!" Clara whines and then storms off. Kelsey and I hold back our giggles until she is out of sight. Then all we hear is the murmur of voices down the hallway as Clara fills her dad in on what her mother just did.

"She's a daddy's girl, all the way," Kelsey says, her smile fading slowly. "Now tell me why you're here and why my child thinks you need lessons on how to apply your makeup."

I sigh. I was enjoying the distraction. It was nice to forget about my life, even if it was for only five minutes. If anything, though, at least she was able to make me stop crying.

"I didn't get the job," I tell her.

"What?" Her whole body leans back. "How is that even possible?"

I shrug, not knowing where to begin, but somehow, I do.

And I don't stop till she knows the entire story. Even the part where I'll be leaving for my mom's as soon as I can. Leaving might not be what I want, but it might be what I need. Those were Kelsey's words, not mine. I really hope she's right.

CHAPTER TWENTY

Maverick

I hate not knowing what I should do right now. Do I keep trying to reach her? Do I wait for her to come to me? What if that never happens? I can't just let her go. Our relationship definitely wasn't perfect, but that doesn't mean I want her out of my life. If anything, it means I want her in my life more. And that's the plan. Find a way to help her understand before she writes me out forever. Show her I'm not giving up.

I glance out the window from my spot behind the wheel. The last time I came here, I had to beg her to let me in and I even attempted to use work as an excuse. Now, though, there is no reason for her to let me through her front door. I could plead a hundred as to why she should, but she's so stubborn, I'll need at least a thousand more just to convince her to let me stand in the doorway. I'd tell her two thousand if it means she'll talk to me.

Before I can let myself think too much more on the matter,

I head for the welcome mat. It's been more than a week since the fiasco at MM. I can't believe I waited this long.

I've barely got three knocks in before the door swings open. Abby stands in front of me in nothing but a t-shirt that hangs off her shoulder. Her arms are crossed and there is a crease between her eyes as she scowls at me. My first reaction is to step back, but I don't because then Tyler steps up behind her. The pity smile he gives me is the complete opposite of Abby's.

"I need to talk to Beth," I say.

"She isn't here."

"Abby, please."

"She isn't here," she repeats.

"I understand if she doesn't want to see me, but I can't not try."

"Maybe you should just stop doing shithead things and then you wouldn't have to try so hard," Abby says.

She's right. But she's also not the person I should be talking to right now.

"She really isn't here, man," Tyler says, opening the door wider for me.

"Since when are you allowed to let people into my apartment?" Abby snaps at him.

"Since he clearly needs someone to talk to and normal fucking people are there for their friends."

"Oh my god. I am not having this conversation with you again. You can both leave!"

Abby storms off to her room, slamming the door. Tyler grabs his coat off the rack and steps out the door like it's the most normal thing in the world for her to yell at him.

"Abby sort of told me what happened, but I'm sure your

side is different," he says. We make it outside the apartment building door when Abby comes out behind us.

"Let's go get coffee," she says to me. She rolls her eyes like Beth does at me as she looks at Tyler. Now I'm wondering who taught whom, or if it's a natural woman thing. "You can come, but this is only to talk about Beth and Maverick. All other subjects are off limits no matter what I say. Got it?"

"Sure thing," Tyler agrees.

I follow behind them as we walk toward the coffee shop.

"So what were you planning to say to Beth when you got here?"

"Where is she?" I ask instead of answering.

"She's with her mom, jackass. You should know that."

"Already?"

"Yeah, she left the day after you ruined her."

That hurt.

"When will she be back?" I ask.

"No clue."

"She's your roommate; she didn't tell you?"

"Maybe."

"Abby, just tell him," Tyler says.

"No, he doesn't deserve to know."

"Well, tell me where her mom lives. I'll go to her there," I say.

Abby laughs. "Yeah, right. So you can make things worse."

"I'm trying to make things better. A little help would be nice."

"You don't deserve nice."

I stop walking. Talking to Abby is pointless. She isn't going to help me.

"I'll be back tomorrow," I say and turn back for my truck.

"For what?" she shouts.

"To ask again."

"I won't tell you."

"Then I'll keep coming back until you do."

She doesn't say anything more after that. I get inside my truck and head for my place. On second thought, I head for the BA. Someone is bound to help a guy out.

I'm about to go inside when I my father's name pops up on my cell.

"Dad, did you find something?" I ask. We've been waiting to hear back from security about the tapes we are having reviewed. They've had to replay some of them more than once. Turns out, what happened to Beth wasn't the only suspicious activity going on at MM. Dad didn't go into detail, he just kept assuring me we'd find something soon.

Since he's decided to stay in Wind Valley till everything is straightened out, his stress level has been going through the roof. I've offered him my help, even if I'm taking some time off, but he doesn't want it. He thinks it's good for me to free up my schedule from the company for a while. What I think he really means is get the girl and then we can talk about where I stand with a job.

His signature drawn-out sigh comes through the phone. "Unfortunately, we did."

Fuck. I lean against my driver door. This doesn't sound good.

"I know you're taking time off, but I'm going to need you

today. Think you can meet me at the office within the next thirty minutes?"

"Of course," I answer.

"I'll see you then," he says and the line goes silent.

Wow.

This really can't be good.

* * *

My father is pacing the lobby when I arrive at the office.

"Dad, what's going on?"

"You know someone your whole life and just when you think they can't give you any more surprises, they pull a move with such betrayal, I don't even know where to begin."

I survey the room around us. No one else is down here.

"Okay …"

Another sigh.

"Just follow me and please understand that what I'm about to do is something I wish I would never have to do," he says.

One elevator ride later and we're standing in my uncle's office with him and Austin.

"Explain yourself," my father's voice booms as the giant folder in his hands lands on Bart's desk with a loud smack.

My uncle looks between me and my father. He doesn't touch the stack of papers before he says, "I told you once, Bill, Maverick isn't fit for this company."

Bart steps to the side of his desk and sits on the corner. "Do you need me to go into detail?"

"Cut the shit," my father snaps and the room goes silent.

Dad's swearing. That's it.

I grab the folder and start flipping through it. Screenshots of Bart and the woman from Colorado. The one I slept with. The one who landed me in the recruitment program. There are snapshots of him handing her a small, white envelope.

Next I find pictures of him stealing money from the receptionist's desk. And of him in my office. I glance to the date. July 2. The same day the email was sent out to the women who arrived at the Fourth of July event.

My hands move quicker until I find what I'm looking for —the shot of him leaving a yellow folder on my desk and the one of him sitting at Beth's computer just hours before our presentation.

Bart took the photos. Holy Shit. I don't even want to know how. I just can't believe it was him.

I set the folder back on his desk and step back, swallowing as I clench my fists and refraining from looking at him. I will hit him if I see his face.

This entire time, I thought this was all Austin's doing, but it wasn't. It was Bart.

"Explain," my father demands again and our attention turns to the door. Austin stands there looking just as guilty.

"Bill, I needed you to see that Maverick isn't fit to lead this company," Bart says. His voice sounds desperate.

"You set me up to fail!" I yell. "You hurt people and ruined careers for what? So you could have some control?"

"I should be the next president in line at this company. Not you!"

"Enough!" my father cuts us both off. "I had Ann pull the numbers, Bart. The amount of money you have stolen could land you in jail for a long, *long* time." He eyes my cousin. "I have no doubt that being an accomplice wouldn't be much less."

Bart takes a step toward my father and I take a step toward him. "You're going to put your own brother in jail?" he asks.

"If that's the only choice you leave me."

Bart lets out a huff as he grabs his coat off his chair and heads for the door where Austin is still waiting.

"I will expect your resignation letter in my email first thing in the morning," Dad says.

The room falls eerily quiet once Dad and I are alone.

"A little warning would have been nice," I say, attempting to lighten the mood.

He smiles, but it doesn't last long. "This was supposed to be a family business."

"Tiff still works here." My sister will be dying to hear what happened.

"And you." He looks up. "This office will need someone to replace your uncle. I couldn't imagine a better fit."

"What? Dad, you just—"

"I know. But I've also never felt more confident that knowing you are the best fit as vice president of Mitchell Marketing."

My blood pumps through my veins. And there is one person I want to share this news with more than anything.

"Can I think about it?" I ask.

He nods and I head for the door.

"Where are you going?" he asks.

"I have a phone call to make."

Beth

The teakettle screams over the stove and I rush to switch it to another burner before the noise wakes my mother. This is my life now. Tea. I make it at least four times a day.

Drinking this soothing hot water is the only thing keeping me sane. Especially when my mother is livid with me and yells every time she looks at me. I'm the devil child who abandoned her and who supports my father's new engagement. Yep, he's engaged. My mother thinks I know because I keep in touch with my father, but really, I know because of Facebook. His fiancée and I are friends. Although I'm not so sure how far you could go calling us that when we met once in person and the remainder of our interaction is on social media.

Mom thinks I have a close relationship with my father. She's wrong about that, too. I haven't spoken to him in more than a year.

I sip the warm liquid and sit on the couch. I've had plenty of time to think here. Plenty of time to put my thoughts together.

It should bother me that my relationship with my family isn't the average American ideal. We don't call or text each other daily to stay in touch and we don't plan events so that we can see each other. No one, expect maybe my brother, even knows what I went to school for. That's my normal world, and after watching the way Maverick acted just to please his father, I can't deny that my way isn't such a bad way to live life.

"Beth!" Her shrill voice makes my skin crawl, but she's Mom. And even if she's going to scream at me for the next hour, I'll let her. Eventually she will grow used to not drinking and maybe one day she'll even thank me for it.

"Hey, Mom, how was your nap?" I ask.

"Same as it was yesterday when you asked and the day before that and the day before that," she answers.

"Well, then I'd say you should be pretty well rested by now." I mean it as a joke, but I don't think she heard it that way.

"Huh, you think you're so smart," she says. It's full of sarcasm, but for the first time this week, at least she isn't yelling.

"On some things," I say, looking away as I smile. I don't know why I have to make it worse on myself.

"No, you're not," she says.

"Mom, can I get you something?" I ask. I don't really feel like sitting here to listen to her tell me how dumb I am.

"You can tell me why you're here. Then maybe I'll know why you made such a dumb decision to come here."

"I'm here because you need me," I say.

"No, no, don't give me that answer."

"I don't have another one."

"Since the minute you got here, you've done nothing but mope. I'm sad, but I look nothing like you."

All I can do is stare at her. We can lose touch, but she still knows how to read me. Telling her I'm here because naked pictures of me were sent around the office where I was trying to get a permanent job, which resulted in me not so pleasantly being asked to leave the building, isn't something I want to talk to her about. And I sure as fuck am not going to tell her it's all because of a boy. She's a drunk because my father left her. Anything she would have to say to me wouldn't help the situation.

"Well, I'll try to look happier," I say and force a smile.

"And I'll try to believe you." She leans back on her bed and closes her eyes. I take this as my cue to leave.

"Beth," she says. Her eyes are still closed.

"Yes?"

"A man can only control your heart for so long. Don't let it go on as long as I did. And if you love him, make it work. Don't lose it all because you're too afraid of what might happen."

She rolls to her side, giving me her back. I close the door but keep looking at the handle.

Every person has a story and right now, I'm figuring out that I never asked my mother what hers is. Maybe tomorrow. That's when I'll take the first step to mend our relationship. And maybe reconsider another.

I head down the hallway, my phone buzzing on the kitchen table drawing my attention. The number is one I don't recognize.

"Hello?"

"Hello, is this Beth Moyer?"

"Yes," I say cautiously to the unfamiliar voice.

"This is Don Jackson, with TACM. How are you today?"

My body perks up and I stop walking toward the living room.

"I'm doing well. How are you?"

Oh my gosh, I sound so lame.

"I'm doing well. Look, I'm contacting you today in regard to the presentation you sent over in an email a couple of days before we met at the MM office."

Shit. Maverick had mentioned sending the presentation to them prior to the meeting. I completely forgot.

"Yes, I—"

"We loved it, although we are a bit surprised that you weren't the one presenting it."

They what?

"There was a mix-up at the office" is all I can think to say.

"That's some mix-up." He laughs. "Still, your work proved to be exactly what we were looking for. We'd like to offer you a position with us, as head of marketing."

"Wow, I don't know what to say. This is amazing, but I didn't put that presentation together by myself."

"Yes, a Maverick Mitchell helped, as it said in the email."

"That's right."

"At this time, we have only one position available."

"I'll take it." The words rush out my mouth.

"Great, we'll be in touch later this week with more details and a potential start date."

"Thank you," I say and hang up.

Wow. I just got a job.

One of the things I've tried to accept since I've been here is that everything happens for a reason. Talk about a girl with a life full of clichés, but sometimes, clichés are real life. It's not the job I first dreamed of, but it's one I know I'll be happy with. Perhaps I wasn't meant to work at MM. And maybe meeting Maverick was what was supposed to show me I didn't belong there.

I sit on the couch and let that sink in. It's not possible. Even after everything, my heart still aches over what I lost with Maverick. I met him because I was supposed to. After that ... well, that was just us messing things up.

CHAPTER TWENTY-ONE

Maverick

Today marks exactly two weeks since the last day I saw Beth.

I spent the entire evening after I found out about my uncle's deception begging Abby, Sky and anyone else at the BA to give me an address or a number where I could reach Beth.

She deserves to know what happened. She needs to know the truth.

Finally, with Tyler's help, Abby gave in.

I pull up in front of a small ranch-style home with a single-car garage. It's faded green with a forest green color for the trim. The grass is dead and there is one tree in the front yard.

I walk up to the door, pausing before I knock when I hear the sound of two women laughing.

I hate to interrupt a good moment, but I'm done waiting to have Beth in my life again.

"One second," Beth's sweet voice hollers through the door at my knock. I hear her approaching and stand tall, shoulders back and head held high.

"Maverick," she says with shock. "What are you doing here?"

"I came to see you," I tell her, although that much is obvious. A wide smile stretches across her face.

"Come in," she says. "I'll make us some tea." The soft words from a voice I've missed the past couple of weeks pulls me in. I follow her into the living room.

"Beth, I—"

"Maverick, this is my mother, June. Mom, this is Maverick," Beth introduces us as she continues to the kitchen.

"Ah, this is him, huh?" June rolls her eyes at me and stands from her spot on the couch. "If my daughter gives you another chance and you hurt her again, I will break you."

"Yes, ma'am," I say, but she has already passed me, headed toward the hallway.

"Here." Beth hands me a white mug and takes her mother's spot on the couch, one leg tucked under the other.

"How are you?" I ask.

"Maverick, small talk, really?"

Setting the cup on the table and sitting next to her I say, "No, I suppose not." I sigh, clearly picking up my father's habits, and run my hands over my face.

"Maverick, just spit it out."

"It was my uncle. All of it. I'm assuming Austin helped, but it was Bart."

"What?"

"He was the one who sent the email from my account and the one from yours, and he is the one who deleted the presentation. He was struggling to accept my advancement in the company."

"Wow."

I scoot closer to her and take her hand. "I hope you know I would never—"

"I know." She cuts me off.

"Beth, these past couple of weeks I've felt … lost. My life without you, it's not right."

She squeezes my hand in hers.

"It's not easy for me to admit when I'm wrong," she says, "but it's very clear in our situation that I may have overreacted. I should have let you speak the day everything blew up in the office. I should have answered at least one of your calls when you tried to reach me. I made a lot of mistakes." She pauses. "And I'm learning. I know I'm not the easiest person to get along with. I know I have always had this image of what relationships are like, but … you changed that view for me."

"How could I change your view if we still ended up apart?"

"You changed it because every day we aren't together, I feel like I'm going to die because I don't see your face, feel your touch, or hear your voice."

My chest swells, and for the first time in the last month, I feel my heart race again.

"Let's give this one more chance," I say.

"Maverick, I know what I just said, but—"

"Don't think about what could happen. Don't think about what has happened to other people. I made mistakes, too, but I swear to you I have learned and I will be better. I know because everything you just said? I feel it too. Don't give up on us. I love you, Beth."

"I'm scared," she whispers as I wipe away the tear that has fallen over her cheek.

"Me, too. But only of losing you."

"So, you want it all?" she asks.

"A real try," I say. "All in—exclusive and everyone knows about us. My family, your family, all our friends. This time, we do this the right way."

Her silence freezes my heart as I wait.

"Okay," is the only word she speaks before I have her face in my hands and my lips pushed against hers.

God, I've missed her.

"I never thought I would live in Montana, let alone in Colorado," she says and I laugh.

"I didn't take the job in Colorado," I tell her.

"You didn't? Are you and your father …?"

"We're good. He's actually looking forward to the day where he can officially meet you and apologize for everything that happened."

"Well, I look forward to the day when we can all forget this."

"Me too, babe, me too."

"So did human resources offer you the job in Wind Valley?"

"No, they offered it to Austin."

"Are you kidding me?"

"No, but then my dad and I reviewed the tapes to find the real answers, and we got more than we wanted. You are now looking at the new, vice president of Mitchell Marketing."

"What?"

"Yeah, it looks like I'll be staying in Wind Valley." I pull her in for a kiss. "And you know, now that my uncle and cousin are gone, there is another position to fill. It's yours if you want it."

"Maverick."

"I'm serious."

"Well, that's awfully sweet of you, but I got a job."

"You did? With who?"

"With TACM."

"That's amazing, but you know you are always welcome at MM."

"I think we both know that working together isn't the best idea."

I kiss her forehead.

As long as I have her, she can work wherever she wants.

<h1 style="text-align:center">EPILOGUE</h1>

Six Months Later …

Beth

The last thing I want to be is cheesy, but spotting Maverick as he walks through the door at the BA, I truly know I am the luckiest woman there is. He's already ditched his jacket, but he's still dashing as ever in his heather-gray suit. He scans the room, and his entire face lights up with just a smile when he finds me. It's probably a natural reaction to the shit-eating grin I know I'm sporting right now. The smile hasn't left my face since he called me an hour ago to let me know he would be off early and suggest we meet here for drinks.

Working for a firm has always been my goal, but I have the perfect job as head of marketing at what is currently the fastest-growing radio station in the state. The day they called me was a good day. It was also the day my mother agreed to seek professional treatment.

I'd love to work each day with Maverick, but if I'm

honest, we both get a whole hell of a lot more done at work when we aren't together.

"Babe, you look incredible," he says, leaning down to press his lips against mine as he slides into the booth. His kiss is over too soon. If we were alone, it'd be a different story.

"Congratulations, Maverick. You've done pretty well for yourself, even with all the distractions these last few months." There's humor to Abby's tone and I know exactly what she's implying.

Maverick's and my relationship is going great. So great, in fact, that when my lease is up at the end of May, I'll be moving into Maverick's apartment. It's weird to think I was the one always losing roommates and now it's Abby who will need to find someone to replace me. She tells me she'll be fine because two jobs will take care of everything financially, but we'll see.

The fact that Maverick and I aren't living together at this point means a lot of sleep-overs. This is what Abby means by distractions. Although, I think it's more of a distraction for her than anyone.

I'm pretty sure she and her latest fling are on the rocks, because she has been home a lot more lately. I think it's good for her.

"I'll gladly take a distraction if it includes this beautiful face," he says, shooting me a wink.

"Awe, that is so cute," Sky says. She's all about the romance world right now, what with the diamond Luke put on her left hand last week. She hasn't been able to stop smiling and now she thinks everyone should fall in love.

"Ugh, gag me" is Abby's response with a roll of her eyes. She slides out of the booth and heads for the bar. Sky follows behind her, leaving me and Maverick alone. He scoots in and wraps an arm around me.

"I can't wait to get you home," he whispers into my ear before placing a long, slow kiss on my lips. "Show you how much I love you."

"Well, then you should have told me to meet you at your place if you wanted to find out how much I love you back," I tell him.

"Who I Am With You" by Chris Young comes on the juke box and Maverick pulls me from the booth, twirling me on the floor before wrapping his arms around my waist to pull me in snugly.

"I can't wait until you're all moved in," he says as we sway back and forth.

"It'll be here sooner than you think, only a few months to go."

He kisses my forehead.

"Make that someday tomorrow. Then I can marry you and we can start a family and begin the rest of our lives, together. No more waiting."

Not even a minute into the song, I move back and stare up at him. He's becoming a pro with all his bluntness. I knew he wanted to be with me, but I never imagined he dreamed up a life for us. He swallows and the large bob of his throat makes it clear he's preparing himself for whatever I have to say next.

"Okay," I say, quicker than I expect. "I want all that, too."

Maverick picks me up in a big hug, lifting my feet off the ground. He spins and I squeal as he sets me down and kisses me.

I can't predict our future and I don't intend to try, but

meeting Maverick sparked something inside me and that feeling, well, I'm never letting it go.

***

Want exclusive content delivered right to your inbox from Jami? Subscribe to her mailing list for exclusive bonus epilogues and all the book news!

Keep reading with book 6, Just One Love, today!

JUST ONE LOVE
CHAPTER ONE

Abby

Slashing someone's tires doesn't make you crazy, does it? Maybe a little.

What if they deserve it? I mean, let's say your boyfriend cheated on you with another woman. That might not be reason enough, but what if, just last night, he told you he loved you? Ding, ding, ding, we have a motive!

All I've wanted in life is to fall in love. True, deep, passionate, real love. The love you only see in movies or read about in books. I want a man who is going to pick me first. A guy who smiles when the first thing he sees is me as he wakes up, and recognizes how lucky he is to be with me. Someone who thinks about me all day, who can't wait to see me the moment he comes home. Someone who makes me happy, who I can trust, and who won't take advantage of me when I give him the same. The list of what I want is long, and right now, in my life, this man doesn't exist. He never has, and I'm not sure he ever will.

Instead, I'm stuck with reality. Hence slashing tires.

"Remind me again why I'm here?" Beth pulls her green Nitro to a stop along the curb.

I glance over to the one friend who has been there for me through all my bad decisions in the last few years. And there are a lot. She deserves a prize or something. Her loyalty to me has been the best, and it's the exact reason she is here right now. I needed someone I could trust to come with me.

The stars provide the minimal glow that I need, and, thankfully, the wind is calm, offering the picture-perfect summer night. The street lamps are dim, and because it's getting late, the houses that line the street all look to be closed down for the evening, with porch lights the only signs someone is home. Everything would be perfect if it weren't for one house. The one I specifically need to not have every single light on.

"I need support," I tell her.

The light from the windows helps display the perfectly manicured lawn and the flowerbeds that sit under the two front windows on each side of the front door. I don't remember their names, but the flowers looks like the hair off the toy trolls. *I should dig them up and take them home with me.*

"Abby, I know better than anyone else that you do not need support to break up with a guy." She sighs and pulls her keys from the ignition.

I slide out of the passenger's seat and gently click the door closed.

This time I might.

Beth slams her door.

"Hey, shhh," I whisper, my arms flailing around like I'm trying to catch the noise and hide it or something.

Last night, around this same time, after my shift at The Black Alcove, the bar I work at, I came here to surprise my boyfriend Jace—and, you guessed it, I caught him with another girl … naked. He doesn't know that I saw. His roommate, on the other hand, who owns the house and who happens to be Tyler Maron—my ex-best friend and the man who holds fifty percent of the blame on why my life turned out the way it did—caught me running to my car. I made him promise not to tell Jace. Which was easy, considering he's always trying to "repair our friendship," as he calls it.

Ugh.

Okay, tonight is not about me and Tyler. It's about Jace and what he deserves.

Revenge is way better than confronting him. Plus, when I think of it as revenge, I feel like it knocks my crazy factor down a notch. Which, technically, I don't think I'm crazy. I just prefer to show my emotions differently than others do.

"I'm just not sure how he's going to react," I say, and it's the honest truth. Most girls would go batshit insane on the other woman. Not me. In my mind, Jace is at fault here. He is the one in the relationship, and he is the one who should have said no.

I crouch down, pretending to rub my legs warm to be sure he doesn't see me and also so Beth doesn't catch on right away what I'm really up to. "Please come with me?"

"Fine," Beth groans. "But this better go fast, because Maverick is at home waiting for me."

Of course she brings up her fiancé. Every one of my friends in Wind Valley has settled down but me. It's like a constant reminder of where my life should be right now. The worst part: in two minutes, I'm about to backtrack. Maturity isn't my strength these days. Well, not when it comes to making a decision for my own life, anyway.

Jace's lifted black and chrome truck is parked right out front, one tire propped up on the curb like your regular jack-ass. We have to walk past it to get to the front door.

This is it, Abby. Don't back out now.

"So, what are you … oh my god, what are you doing? Is that a knife? That thing is …" Beth stops mid-sentence when I jam a hunting knife into the back tire of Jace's truck.

"Ahh! Holy crap!" I scream whisper. I grab my right wrist as pain shoots toward my elbow and glare at Beth as the knife rattles off the sidewalk. Beth's bent over laughing.

"Did you plan for it to go *into* the tire?"

"Yes." I try not to laugh. "Now be quiet or they are going to hear you." I sneak a glance at the front window. No movement and the lights are still on. This is good.

I grab the knife and begin round two.

"Abby, stop, you can't be serious. You could get in trouble for this; *we* could get in trouble for this." She's got her hands on her hips now, acting like a total buzzkill.

"I'm extremely serious." I hike up my leg and immediately feel the handle of the knife through the bottom of my flip-flop. The knife doesn't budge. Gripping the bed of the truck, I pull myself up until I'm standing on his tire. Then, I repeatedly bounce on the knife—ignoring Beth, who is now tugging on the back of my shirt and yelling at me to get down —until I hear the smooth hiss of air leaking from the tire.

Success!

"Abby, get down. I hear someone."

My neck pops as I jerk it around at the familiar noise. Jace and Tyler are walking outside, talking loudly. Tyler's voice grows as if he were right next to me. I peek over the bed of the truck, and Tyler's eyes meet mine briefly. Then they do a double take.

"Man, let's wait another hour before we hit up the bar. It's early, no one goes this early."

"It's after ten, Tyler. How much longer do you want to wait?" Jace asks, continuing for his truck.

Shit!

I jump down and grab my knife, but as I pull back in what should be the segue into my quick getaway run—dramatic, smooth, commanding, just like in the movies—I'm jerked back.

Shit. Shit. Shit.

The knife is stuck.

"Abby, let's go!" Beth snaps at me. She's crouched behind the truck where they can't see her. "I cannot believe that I trusted that you were going to break up with him like a normal person. Let's go."

"I'm trying," I shush back, jerking again on the damn knife.

"Just leave it."

"It has my initials on it."

A gift from my mom for my eighteenth birthday. She knows me so well. *Not.*

"What the ... seriously?" Beth moves around to the tire and pushes me out of the way. I duck when Jace's ball cap comes into view over the back of the truck. Then, Beth and I yank on the knife together.

Nothing happens.

"Let me drive!" Tyler shouts.

"Dude, what the fuck is your deal? It's my truck. I'll drive."

"But I'm thinking of getting one just like it, and I need to test drive something." Tyler's response is quick.

"Dude, whatever," Jace replies as I see the keys flying through the air, right before Tyler comes into view.

"What the fuck are you doing, Abby?" he says through the side of his lips. I barely see his mouth move.

"Trying to leave. What does it look like?" I whisper frantically.

"Whoops!" Tyler drops the keys. He kneels in front of the tire and jerks the knife out in one swift move.

Damn.

His white T-shirt hugs his bicep, and, oh boy, he looks good tonight. I mean, he's always had the whole Liam Hemsworth thing going on, but tonight he looks even hotter than a movie star. His hair is the perfect dirty blonde and his eyes are brightest green I've ever seen. Don't even get me started on his smile. Shoot, any girl would agree to whatever he wanted just to see it one more time. I would know. I've been that girl.

Tyler gives the knife to me and mouths "run." We don't hesitate in the slightest.

I tuck the knife into my back pocket as I duck to run. The tire is successfully slashed, and I'm not leaving any evidence of my crime at the scene.

Hunching behind her car, Beth shoots daggers from her eyes as she stares at me. The look is so intense, I need something else to focus on.

Yes, this crack on the sidewalk is a nice distraction.

"I can't believe you," she seethes.

"It's fine. No one saw us but Tyler," I say just as Jace begins shouting a string of curses.

Jackass.

"I should have known you were going to do something crazy tonight. You made breaking up sound so simple," Beth adds.

I shrug and then we both hunker down tighter when the lights of Tyler's truck flash our way. I crawl around the front of the car and watch them turn the corner.

Then, I start to laugh.

Beth is still glaring at me. Only now she's standing with her hands on her hips and looking at me like my mom would when I'd come home past curfew, before she decided she didn't want anything to do with me.

The whole picture makes me laugh even harder. Slowly, Beth's lips begin to tug into a smile.

"You are out of control," she says and unlocks her car.

"There is nothing wrong with that," I tell her.

With the click of my seat belt, she pulls onto the road. "Back to the BA?" she asks.

I nod.

"Oh man," she says, releasing a long breath. "I forgot how quickly hanging out with you could go from a zero to a ten in less than five seconds."

"I like to keep it interesting."

"Yeah, but …"

"But what?" I ask.

"Doesn't it feel a bit … high school-ish?"

"No, he cheated on me. I think it's justified."

"Well, maybe if you dated someone who was not a jackass

and who cared less about the fingerprints on his truck and more about say, opening a door for you, you would see it differently."

"Eh, I don't know."

"Come on, Abby. You'd rather keep doing this than have a real relationship? Settle down? Fall in love?"

It's not as easy as she makes it sound. She knows my life. I'm not exactly the type that screams "settle down with me and take me home to your mom." Shit, once I confess about my mom to the guy I'm dating, he usually disappears within a week.

"I'm not trying to be mean. I'm just saying, a situation like the one we just created makes me even more thankful that I have Maverick," she says.

I roll my eyes.

"You were so much cooler before you met him." I nudge her arm.

"Yeah, but I wouldn't trade anything for what I have now," she says.

"What, a fiancé?"

"Yes, but also good friends, a job I actually want to be at, and a life filled with happiness and love."

I nod slowly. "Are you the new spokesman for the Hall-mark Channel?" I ask.

Beth shakes her head. "God, I have no idea how you do it."

"Do what?"

"Stay the same old Abby I've known since we graduated high school. I mean, you've yet to date a guy who actually cares about you," she says just as her cell phone rings. She presses a button on the steering wheel and Maverick's voice fills the car.

I'm not the same old Abby.

I've changed.

Haven't I?

I cross my arms and stare out the window as we near the BA.

If I'm not at home, I'm at the BA. You'd think that since I work there, I'd never want to hang out there. You'd also think that, given my reputation, I wouldn't want to socialize with the people who spend their time there. I've hurt more than one of them and, yet, they still keep me around, which is just crazy because I've never …

Oh my god.

I glance over to Beth, who's still chatting away as she takes the last turn onto the bar's street.

I've never done anything except let them down. Whether it was my choices or actions, I haven't been a good friend. Or person in general, it seems.

Maybe Beth is right.

I'm the same old Abby.

My cell lights up with an incoming text. Tyler. I flip it over just as Beth says goodbye to Maverick.

"Do you think it's too late?" I ask her.

"For what?"

"To change."

She must gather that I'm referring to my life and not something lame like our clothes, because she doesn't answer right away.

She pulls into a parking space and turns off her car. "It's never too late," she says.

She shoots me wink before she gets out. I follow, but I don't think I'll go inside. My mind is racing from our short conversation.

I'll always wonder if, on that day, I'd found the strength to say no, to reject the boy I fell in love with at thirteen and who used to be my best friend, how different my life would be right now.

Maybe I'd still have all my girlfriends, and everyone who used to invite me to parties or movies wouldn't think of me as trouble. Maybe I'd have had a roommate those first couple years out of school rather than still living with my mom and maybe I wouldn't have … it doesn't matter. What's done is done, but what I do know is this: I need to make some changes.

Tyler

You only get one real best friend in life, and once you find them, you should do whatever you can to keep them.

Damn.

I wish someone had told me this right out of high school instead of letting me figure it out on my own.

The cell phone vibration in my pocket wakes me up enough to pay a bit more attention to the real estate meeting I'm in this morning. I'd like to blame my lack of energy today on staying out too late with Jace, since he's moving back to California today, but that's not it. I was thinking about Abby.

She was my best friend. Then I messed up. *We* messed up.

Every now and then, Abby and I can be civil, but somehow it ends with us in an argument. We then don't speak for a while, I try to make it better, Abby has her quick, snappy responses, and eventually we start talking again … and start the process all over.

She has no idea how much I'd kill to regain the type of friendship we had growing up. She's the only person I trusted, and as crazy as it sounds, she still is.

I sit up straighter in my chair and glance around the room as I pretend to be taking notes. For the last three years, I've sold more homes than anyone sitting at this table. That includes Rob, and he's been here for almost a decade.

"Let's move on to our next topic," Marshall Jinks, my boss, says and flops open a giant, red, three-ring binder in front of him as he sits at the head of the rectangle table.

I'm glad they're changing the subject since I have no idea what the last one was. I really hope it wasn't anything that pertained directly to me.

"The office in Colorado."

Yes.

He's been talking about this location for months. He hasn't come right out and said it, but I'm pretty sure he's going to pick someone from this office to lead the new one.

It's a challenge I'm ready to accept. I've earned it. Each house I sell, I'm selling a family a fresh start. It's my turn, and moving to Colorado, or anywhere, and managing my own team is how that's going to happen. It's all part of my plan. Being my own boss and being in control is at the top of the list.

He's got my undivided attention. "As most of you know, I'd like to train the new agents in this office and move them to Colorado once the building is complete at the end of the summer. With only a few months till that deadline, it's time I share my plans with everyone."

Say you want someone from this office.

"I would like to promote one of my agents here to lead the Colorado office."

Yes! Fuck. Yes. If there weren't a group of people sitting near me, I'd definitely being doing a victory dance right now, but I'll have to settle for a clap with the rest of the group for now.

"Choosing this candidate isn't going to be an easy choice. There are many of you here who qualify for this position and who I would be honored to call my partner."

I survey the fifteen of us around the table. Who else could he be considering? I mean, Macy, maybe. She sold one only less house than me last year. Carl could be picked; he's really good at bringing clients in to the company, and Sandy—well, Sandy is the boss's sister-in-law.

"I'm not going to do a competition or something crazy to pick this person. Just continue working hard and remember that I notice all your hard work."

That's it?

"Now, next up," he says, and I lean back, the creak of my chair in unison with everyone else who clearly feels the way I do.

That's seriously all he's going to say about the promotion?

"We have a full schedule for company events over the next six weeks. As you all know, we market ourselves on our community involvement. I don't want the idea of a possible promotion to detour us from this."

How could it? Everyone could handle the company events in their sleep. Park picnics, fancy dinners out, a work banquet. It's not like the company gets too crazy.

"This year, things are going to be a bit different." Again,

Mr. Jinks has my full attention. "Along with a few of the same good ole times, we'll be hosting a fundraiser and going on a weekend getaway to a cabin near the Colorado office. A lot of that market is about the great outdoor living that the state has to offer, so I want to make sure everyone is fully prepared. I also want to introduce ourselves to the surrounding community in that region."

"You're bringing all of us?" Macy asks, her eyes roaming the room.

"Yes," he answers. "You're all my top agents, and it's time you are rewarded for it."

"That's … wow … this is a great idea. Genius," Carl says, and I want to roll my eyes. He's always kissing the boss's ass. Don't get me wrong—we all do it from time to time, but he's the worst.

To be honest, I'm the youngest of the bunch at twenty-five, and not to be stereotypical, but you'd think I'd be the one saying or doing cheesy shit to get the boss's attention. Lucky for me, I keep my age in mind and speak only after I've fully thought out what to say.

"Thank you, Carl." Mr. Jinks smiles proudly. "I really want us to stand out against the other agencies in town. If anyone has ideas, I'm open to them all."

"We could give something away," Macy says. "People are always drawn to free stuff."

"It could be something like a free shampoo cleaning with every purchase," Sandy chimes in.

Yeah, because every person would rather buy a brand-new house than to just spend sixty bucks and hire someone to clean the carpets they already own.

"That's brilliant," Carl adds.

I hold up my pen as if I'm raising my hand. I hate to interrupt their *brilliant* idea.

"Tyler, do you have something to add?" Mr. Jinks asks.

"Not really," I say, and Macy glares at me. "I was actually thinking we could do something more personal for our clients."

I say the words carefully when what I really want to say is "something that doesn't bribe people to come to us."

"Go on."

"Everyone in Wind Valley knows we can sell them a house …"

"Obviously." Carl snickers and shakes his head. "Tell us something we don't know, Maron."

I side-eye Carl but don't reply. "What we should be doing is selling them a home. A life. A new beginning. Showing them that this house, a new house, is the start to family memories and years of happiness."

Carl, Macy, and Sandy stare at me. Sandy sits up straight in her chair and taps her pen on the table.

"I actually think his idea would be a better approach," she says.

"Yeah, but how do we do that?" Carl asks.

"Easy," Mr. Jinks cuts in, and all eyes are on him. "I want all the events this year to be family-oriented. Bring your wives, husbands, girlfriends, boyfriends, kids, brothers, whoever. Every event will be about family. I love it."

He begins to gather his notebook, cellphone, and snaps his pen into his front shirt pocket. "You've got quite the view on this market, Tyler. Don't let go of it," he says right before he walks out of the room.

All eyes turn to me briefly before most everyone takes

their belongings and return to their offices. Carl stays behind to walk out with me.

"You are the last person I'd have expected to take the family route on this, Tyler," he says, lingering in the doorway and causing me to stop.

"Why is that?" I ask.

"Isn't it obvious?" His brows dip. Guess it's clear that it's not. "You're the only single guy at the firm, Tyler."

He smirks and, with an arrogant laugh, leaves me standing in the hall outside the conference room.

Did I just set myself up?

As I pass cubicle after cubicle down the hall to my office, I notice one thing: every person has pictures of their families on their desks.

I don't even own a dog. Shit.

If Mr. Jinks wants family and I don't have anyone other than my parents, well, maybe I need to change that. Maybe I need to get me a temporary something to get me through these events.

I take a seat behind my desk. Today's schedule is booked full. My performance will overlook my lack of family. I don't need to go getting crazy with a fake girlfriend.

"Tyler." Mr. Jinks pops into my office.

"Yes, sir?"

"I'm looking forward to meeting your other half." He grins. "I assume that's what sparked your sudden interest in family values."

So, as of this moment, I'm in a relationship.

"Yes, sure, she'll be thrilled to hear the news as well," I say.

Mr. Jinks slaps the doorframe and leaves.

Good.

My day just got even busier. I have houses to sell and a girlfriend to find.

Keep reading Just One Love today!

Don't want to miss out on any new releases from Jami? Subscribe to her mailing list for exclusive bonus epilogues and all the book news!

MORE BOOKS BY JAMI ROGERS

The Black Alcove Series

Just One Kiss

Just One Night

Just One Touch

Just One Moment

Just One Spark

Just One Love

The Kiss Me Crazy Series

Kiss Me Crazy

Love is Crazy

I Want Crazy

The Evergreen Brothers Series

A Boyfriend by Christmas

The Summer Wedding Hoax

A Match by Christmas

The Lust or Bust Series

The Write One

Write About You

The Write Choice

Write That Down

More Than Write

Always Been Write

Standalone Novels

Love Money

Date in the Dark (A New Years Eve Novella)

ACKNOWLEDGMENTS

I believe I say this about every book, but this book was honestly the hardest to write. I say that because planning a wedding and writing a novel at the same time was not an easy task. Yet, somehow, I did it (with a lot of help from my editor) and now Beth's story is out there for all to read. I hope you enjoyed it.

Mom, Dad, and Holly: I'll continue to thank you day after day for the support you have for me. You are my biggest promoters and I love it and you!

Dana: As much as I hate to admit this, I am pretty sure that if it weren't for you, I'd still be writing this book. You pushed me to finish it before I left to be married and because of you, I did. Thank you, thank you!

Julie Sturgeon: You make me a better writer. I couldn't do this without you. The fact you are always there for me when I need you, at any time of day, means so much. We are a team and I wouldn't have it any other way.

Megan Phillips: I am so happy I brought reading back to your life and I love that my books have been a part of it. Thank you for being a beta reader and helping me grow as an author.

Mallori and Kate: Knowing I can count on you during the

final stages of edits is a good feeling. Thank you for being there for me!

Melissa: Thank you for listening to me go on and on about my books as I work out any plot holes. Also, thanks for letting me stick around even when I have to cancel plans last minute because I'm hitting a deadline. You rock!

InkSlinger: You do an amazing job at organizing cover reveals, blog tours, release days, and more! Thank you for helping me spread the word.

Readers and Bloggers: Without you, I wouldn't be publishing my sixth book. You believe in me and my characters and I can never thank you enough.

ABOUT THE AUTHOR

My name is Jami Rogers and I write new adult contemporary and adult contemporary romance novels. I *love* love and want to share my passion for happily ever afters with the world.

I was born in Wyoming and still live in the cowboy state with my husband, daughter, and two dogs. I like to read, write, run, watch movies/TV and spend time with my family. I'm horrible at returning phone calls and prefer to text, but still struggle to hit the little blue arrow to send a message once I'm finished typing my reply. My husband does 90% of the cooking in our house. Not because I'm busy – I'm just simply a bad cook.

Keep up with Jami by visiting her website www. authorjamirogers.com

or

Subscribe to her mailing list for exclusive bonus epilogues and all the book news!

www.ingramcontent.com/pod-product-compliance
Lightning Source LLC
Chambersburg PA
CBHW020022310726
48970CB00007B/2170